Pu[...]
boys are dogs

"Fresh, fun, and full of heart, *Boys Are Dogs* will empower girls while giving them the giggles at the same time."
—Meg Cabot, author of the Princess Diaries and
Allie Finkle's Rules for Girls series

"Sweeties, you *must* read this wonderful book.
IT HAS SO MUCH GREAT ADVICE ABOUT BOYS IN IT!!!!!
All that, and a fabulous, funny, warm-hearted story, too.
Read! Read! Read!!!!" —Lauren Myracle,
bestselling author of *Eleven*, *Twelve*, and *Thirteen*

★ "[An] effervescent story. . . . The story lines—melded household, moving, boys as dogs—coalesce naturally, giving girl readers a thoughtful story along with, just possibly, some substantive boy advice."
—*Publishers Weekly*, starred review

"This clever and humorous premise is deftly handled to create a believable and enjoyable tale with a likable and resourceful heroine whose trials, tribulations, and triumphs will have others wanting a training manual of their own." —*SLJ*

"Margolis has created the ultimate must-read for tweens, packed full of fantastic advice, laughs, and a bunch of confidence-boosting girl-power."
—TheCompulsiveReader.com

boys are dogs

books by
leslie margolis

Boys Are Dogs

Girls Acting Catty

boys are dogs

leslie margolis

BLOOMSBURY

NEW YORK BERLIN LONDON

For Jim, who's like a dog
in only the best of ways

Copyright © 2008 by Leslie Margolis
First published by Bloomsbury U.S.A. Children's Books in 2008
Paperback edition published in 2009

Published by Bloomsbury U.S.A. Children's Books
175 Fifth Avenue, New York, New York 10010

The Library of Congress has cataloged the hardcover edition as follows:
Margolis, Leslie.
Boys are dogs / by Leslie Margolis.—1st US. ed.
        p.   cm.
Summary: When her mother gets a new boyfriend, sixth-grader Annabelle
gets to cope with a new town, a new school, and a new puppy and, while
training her puppy, she decides to apply some of the same techniques to
tame the unruly boys that are making her middle-school life miserable.
ISBN-13: 978-1-59990-221-0 • ISBN-10: 1-59990-221-4 (hardcover)
[1. Moving, Household—Fiction. 2. Dogs—Training—Fiction. 3. Interpersonal
relations—Fiction. 4. Middle schools—Fiction. 5. Schools—Fiction] I. Title.
        PZ7.M33568Bo 2008   [Fic]—dc22   2007052362

ISBN-13: 978-1-59990-381-1 • ISBN-10: 1-59990-381-4 (paperback)

Typeset by Westchester Book Composition
Printed in the U.S.A. by Quad/Graphics Fairfield
        4   6   8   10   9   7   5

All papers used by Bloomsbury U.S.A. are natural, recyclable products
made from wood grown in well-managed forests. The manufacturing
processes conform to the environmental regulations of the country of origin.

prologue
the first clue

Before Camp Catalina's first-ever boy-girl dance, all anyone could talk about was the big night. Here's what it sounded like in my bunk. (I could tell you who said what, but there's no point. We all talked like this.)

"We're lucky the boys' camp is coming here. Having the dance on our turf will be so much better."

"What if a boy I don't like asks me to dance?"

"Dance with him, anyway. It's better to dance with a boy you don't like than with no boy at all."

"But what if he's funny looking?"

"It'll be dark."

"What if he smells bad?"

"Bad like he's been chewing on garlic? Or bad like he's just stepped in dog poop?"

"Either one."

"Just make sure to breathe through your mouth and not through your nose."

"Or pretend like you didn't understand the question and run."

We went on like that for three weeks straight.

My bunk was in charge of planning the dance, and we took our job very seriously. We spent three whole days in arts and crafts making a disco ball out of mirrored tiles and a Styrofoam globe. Then we auditioned our five favorite counselors to see who'd make the best DJ.

On the night of the dance, we pushed the cafeteria chairs and tables out of the way to make space for a dance floor. We decorated the room with streamers and decorated ourselves with cool outfits, cherry flavored lip gloss, and glittery eye shadow.

We looked fabulous. Like movie stars, even. The speakers vibrated with a perfect mix of oldies, pop and hip-hop. We tried out our goofy new dance moves, wolfed down pretzels, and sipped punch. It was a blast. Fantastic. Some even called it blast-tastic. But that was all before the boys showed up.

They filed off their bus, messy-haired and slouchy. Every single one of them wore regular old shorts or jeans and ratty T-shirts.

Once inside, they stood in one corner in an unfriendly, lumpy clump. Instead of dancing, they pushed each other around. Rather than eat our food, they threw it at one another. Then they tore down our streamers. Or maybe that happened after their group wrestling match. It's hard to keep track. At some point, a bunch of them snuck out and threw eggs at our cabins. No one realized it until after they'd left, so we got stuck cleaning up their mess.

Those middle school boys acted like a pack of wild dogs. But I didn't know it then. And by the time I figured it out, it was almost too late.

chapter one
a slobbery surprise

Summer was officially over. There would be no more swimming, snorkeling, or bodysurfing in the cool blue waves. No more relay races, and no more circling the campfire to sing songs and toast marshmallows.

For eight whole weeks, the world of school and homework and chores had been replaced with non-stop fun. Sometimes at camp, I smiled so much that by the end of the day my face hurt. But I wasn't smiling now. Our ferryboat from Catalina Island had landed, the parking lot was already crowded with parents, and I just spotted my mom.

"I can't believe this is it," Mia said as we filed off the boat. Her voice sounded strained and her eyes filled with tears. Mia cried last summer when we were only saying good-bye to camp, not good-bye for real.

I'm the one who should have been crying. While I was away at camp, my mom moved in with her boyfriend, Ted. That meant I moved, too.

Sophia huffed out a small breath. "Stop crying," she said. "We'll still see Annabelle next Saturday."

Sometimes Sophia is a little bossy, but Mia and I were used to it. The three of us had been best friends since kindergarten.

I hugged Sophia and said, "I'll miss you."

"Call me when you get there."

"Sure thing," I promised, since it's never a good idea to argue with Sophia.

"As soon as you walk inside."

"Will do."

Next, I hugged Mia, who smelled like bug spray. "Call me right after," she said. "And good luck with Dweeble."

Dweeble is my secret name for Ted. It's only fitting, since his last name is Weeble, and he's the dweebiest guy I know. Example? The first time I met Ted he had a giant spaghetti sauce stain on his shirt. He and my mom had gone out for Italian food, and I guess he spilled. So basically, my mom just moved in with a man who needs to eat with a bib.

They've been together for over a year, but at least they're not getting married—yet. They want to try living together first, to see how it goes. I can tell them right now that it's not going well. Not for me, anyway.

"Bye!" my friends called.

"See you later." I waved back, but it didn't seem right. I said the same thing last summer, when we all knew we'd see each other less than a week later in school. But those days were over now.

When I reached my mom, she bent down and squeezed me tight. "Welcome home, Annabelle."

Her curly blond hair smelled like coconut shampoo. I didn't let go right away because despite it all, I'd missed her, too.

Still, we didn't linger in the parking lot. Mom wanted to get home and I didn't want to start crying. So I said fast good-byes to my counselor, Jane, and to the rest of the girls from my cabin. Then we found my two overstuffed duffel bags and hauled them over to Mom's car.

"Wait until you see the new house. You'll love it," Mom said as we loaded my things into the trunk.

I watched Mia and Sophia head over to Mia's dad's car, at the other end of the parking lot. Their matching dark braids reminded me of the thick rope we used to tie the kayaks to the camp dock.

My hair is blond and straight and too thin to hold a braid. It hardly stays in a ponytail.

"Did you hear me?" asked my mom.

I nodded. "I already saw the new house." Did she forget that she and Ted took me there the week before I left for camp?

"Yes, but now all of our stuff is in it, so it looks even better."

"Mine and your stuff? Or yours and Ted's?"

"All of our stuff," she replied, like it was that simple. "Although there's still plenty of unpacking to do."

"Lucky me," I mumbled.

Mom pretended like she didn't hear. She keeps trying to convince me that the move isn't a big deal. And for her, it's not. The new house is in Westlake, almost thirty miles away from our old apartment. She still gets to have her same job, teaching tenth grade English at North Hollywood High School. Plus, she can drive anywhere she wants. I'm only eleven, and my bicycle is so rusty it squeaks whenever I pedal.

I slouched down in my seat and looked out the window.

"Are those new shorts?" my mom asked.

I fingered the frayed edge of the cutoffs. "Mia let me borrow them because all my stuff was dirty."

"That was nice of her."

I shrugged. "She probably just felt sorry for me."

No comment from my mom, not that I was surprised.

We had a fight about cutoffs before I left for camp. I'm not allowed to make my jeans into shorts. Mom says it's a waste of fabric. If I want shorts, she'll buy me shorts. But if she's going to spend money on jeans, they have to stay jeans.

Now she sighed and said, "Oh, Annabelle. Try and have a good attitude about this. Think of it as a big adventure. You get to go to a new school."

"Where I know no one."

"And we get to live in a house. That's much better than an apartment. Wait until you see the tomato plants I put in the backyard. Soon we'll have fresh vegetables growing in our very own garden. Can you believe it?"

"Tomatoes are a fruit."

I leaned forward and turned on the radio, but Mom kept talking.

"I know you liked St. Catherine's, but this really is for the best."

When I didn't say anything, Mom finally got the hint and stopped talking.

An hour later, we were in the new neighborhood. Too soon, we turned onto Clemson Court, our new street. It's called a cul-de-sac, which is a fancy word for dead end. All the houses around here looked the same. Each had two stories, a redbrick chimney attached to one side, and a square patch of grass out front. There were no stores or gas stations or cool places to walk to—just house after house after identical house.

"Get ready for a surprise," my mom said as we got closer.

Her voice was singsongy, like she had a secret she couldn't wait to tell me. But my mom can't keep secrets, and I'm never surprised. Not on my birthday or even at Christmas. I always know what I'm getting. All I had to do was wait and she'd spill the beans.

Of course, today I didn't even have to wait. I'd already figured out what she got me—a basketball hoop. Two houses on our new street already had hoops above their garages. When I'd first noticed, I asked my mom if I could get one, too. She'd said, "We'll see," in this happy way that made me think she definitely planned on buying me one.

Even though I had to leave my friends behind, a small part of me—maybe the size of my pinky toe—

was excited about having my own driveway where I could shoot hoops. We didn't have our own driveway at the old apartment, just a parking space in a dark underground lot. Sometimes I took my ball to the park, but usually the courts there were filled with guys from the high school—the kind of guys who liked to swear and spit. No way would I ever ask them to share a court.

But when we pulled up to the house, I didn't see a hoop. I figured it must be inside. "Can I draw a half court on the driveway if I use erasable chalk?" I asked. Our new driveway was covered in blacktop, the perfect surface for dribbling. If only it didn't slope so much.

Mom's eyebrows shot up. "Why would you need a half court?" she asked.

"Come on. I know you got me a basketball hoop."

Rather than answer me, she just sighed a little.

And then I knew that I wasn't getting a basketball hoop. That there was some other surprise waiting for me, and for once, my mom wasn't going to give it up.

As we walked inside, my stomach felt fluttery, like it did whenever I got nervous before some big test.

I followed Mom into the kitchen, where we found Dweeble peeling potatoes over the sink. His beard was thicker than how I remembered it, and the bright light from above bounced off his bald head in a way that wasn't exactly attractive.

I didn't want to hug him or anything. It was weird enough seeing him in what was supposed to be *our* kitchen. Yellow tile covered the floors and counter-tops, and I know for a fact that my mother can't stand the color yellow. She thinks it's the most stress-inducing color of the rainbow. When I told her I didn't believe colors could induce stress, she insisted there was scientific research to back it up, and literature, too. But I'll bet she never complained to Dweeble about the color.

"Annabelle. Welcome back. How was camp?" Dweeble's voice seemed too big for the room. He's over six feet tall. I'm short for my age, anyway, but next to Dweeble, I feel extra shrimpy. Luckily, he just stood there, and didn't move in for a hug.

"It was fun," I replied, trying—and failing—to keep from smiling. Camp was way better than just fun, but I didn't feel like gushing.

"We missed you around here."

I wasn't going to lie and say I missed him too, so I stayed quiet. Not bothered by the silence, Dweeble went right on talking. "Wait until you try my famous mashed potatoes. They'll knock your socks off."

"I'm not wearing socks," I told him, pointing to my pale blue flip-flops.

"Well, you're lucky," he replied.

Before I could ask him how any potato could be famous, I heard a strange yelping sound. It seemed to be coming from the back of the house.

"What's that noise?" I asked.

Dweeble turned to my mom and asked, "You didn't tell her, did you?"

"I told you I wasn't going to," she said.

"Yes, but I know how you are about keeping secrets," he teased.

So he knew, too. I didn't like that.

The sliding glass door rattled in its frame, and the noise grew louder. It sounded like something outside was trying to get in. "What's going on?" I asked.

"I'll be right back." Dweeble dropped a soon-to-be-famous potato into a bowl and then walked to the back of the house. A second later I heard the door open and then, very clearly, a bark, which made no sense at all.

Neither did what happened next: a gigantic blur of fur charged at me and jumped up, planting two scruffy paws in the softest part of my stomach. Something wet hit my chin. OOF!

I stumbled and fell on the floor.

The kitchen tile was cold and hard but I barely noticed. Not with this crazy, hyper dog in my lap. Its little pink mouth panted warm, stinky animal breath as it licked my face.

"Get it off!" I said, laughing and holding my hands up to protect my face.

Every time I tried to scramble out of the way the dog moved, too. It just wouldn't leave me alone. Its tongue felt wet and its fur tickled my neck. I couldn't help but giggle.

Dweeble chuckled his dweeby chuckle.

Silly, happy tears streamed down Mom's face. "Surprise!" she cried.

"You got me an attack dog?" I asked, once I finally managed to climb to my feet.

The dog yapped like he was trying to tell me something.

"He's not an attack dog," Mom said. "He's just a puppy. Isn't he adorable?"

The puppy whipped his tail so hard, his whole backside wiggled. His fur was long and shaggy, and mostly black, with some small brown and white patches scattered around. He looked sort of like a tiny, furry cow, but with backward colors.

Mom jumped up and down and clapped little baby claps. "You should have seen your face. It was so hard to keep it a secret. I was dying to tell you the whole way home. But I'm so glad I didn't."

I looked from the dog to my mom.

"You mean we get to keep him?" I asked, crouching down to pet him.

"Of course," she said. "You've been so great about the move. Ted and I decided that this would be a nice thing to do."

The two of them beamed down at me, arm in arm.

She and Ted decided? I didn't like the sound of that.

And what was my mom thinking? We move in with her dweeby boyfriend, and all I get is a dog? Like that's supposed to make up for everything?

"He's part border collie and part Lab, we think," said my mom.

"He might have some bulldog in him, as well,"

Dweeble added. "Look at how large his paws are. That means he's going to be really big."

They both kept talking to fill up the silence, until finally my mom asked, "So what do you think?"

What did I think? I did the math in my head: Mom got a big boyfriend. They moved into this big house, and then found me a big dog. This all stunk of one thing: A Big Bribe.

I stood up. The puppy stared at me with large, honey-colored eyes.

More than anything, I wanted to keep on petting his soft fur, but I resisted. In fact, I tried to not even look at him.

"So?" asked my mom.

I crossed my arms over my chest and did my best to frown. "So does this mean I'm not getting a basket-ball hoop?"

"Oh, honey," said Mom, which I guess meant no.

"This little guy is much better than a basketball hoop," Dweeble tried.

"And you've always wanted a dog," Mom reminded me.

"I have?" I asked.

"Of course. You begged me for one when you were six. Right after your grandmother took you to see *101 Dalmatians*. Remember?" She sounded worried.

"Kind of," I said, even though I really did remember. "I'll bet every kid wants a dog after she sees *101 Dalmatians*. After I saw *Babe* I wanted a pig."

"I've always wanted to get you a dog, Annabelle. You know that. It's just that the old apartment was too small, and now we have this big, fenced-in yard."

Exactly. That big yard totally meshed with my Big Bribe theory.

"We were going to take you to pick one out yourself," said Dweeble. "But when we visited the shelter two days ago your mother fell in love with this guy."

"I just couldn't leave without him. And I wanted to surprise you, too," Mom added.

Not only was I surprised . . . I was also surprised about being surprised. And guess what? It turns out I don't like surprises. Not even cute, fluffy ones.

"You can name him," said Dweeble. "We've been calling him Stripe, but that's just temporary."

"Stripe?" I asked.

"Because he has spots."

I said nothing. Dweeble's smile faded ever so slightly.

"It's supposed to be funny," he said.

If there were an award for the worst sense of humor ever, Dweeble would win first prize. I looked to my mom for help. She patted my shoulder. "You don't have to name him yet. Just think about it."

The dog sniffed at the floor.

Mom crouched down and scratched him behind his ears. "You have to admit he is adorable."

As I looked down at the cute, bouncy ball of fur, my heart went all melty. I didn't mean for it to happen. It's just, well, puppies have that effect on me.

Still, I struggled to hold my ground. It wouldn't be fair, making it that easy for Mom and Dweeble. Yes, they got me a puppy with floppy ears, and a shiny black nose, and a bright pink tongue, and soft fur that I ached to stroke. But that didn't make everything okay. What about my friends? And school? What about my whole life?

Mom stood up. The puppy begged for more attention but I refused to give in. And he must have gotten the idea, because the next thing I knew, he turned around and trotted out of the room.

"Where's he going?" Dweeble asked.

"Don't know." I patted the pockets on my cutoffs. "He gave me a map but I must have misplaced it."

"Very funny," Mom said, as the three of us followed the puppy down the hall.

He moved fast, turning left into the den. We were right on his tail. Well, not literally on his tail, but really close.

Dweeble crouched down and patted his knees. "Come on, little guy. You don't want to stay in here. This room is a mess."

Only Dweeble would try to reason with a dog like he was a person.

Not that Stripe paid him any attention. I was starting to like this little puppy.

"We haven't unpacked in here, yet," my mom explained.

Stripe sniffed at a stack of boxes, then made his way over to a fancy-looking rug with a three-legged table on top. He sniffed the table and then tilted his nose up to sniff the large, leafy plant sitting on its edge.

"Careful!" cried Dweeble. I guess he was scared Stripe would knock over the table. But Stripe didn't. Dweeble did when he lunged forward to shoo Stripe out of the way.

As the table toppled the plant crashed to the floor. The clay pot split open and dirt spilled everywhere.

Startled by the noise, the puppy yelped and ran around in circles. Then he crouched down and peed.

"Not on the Persian rug!" Dweeble cried.

Like Stripe cared where the rug came from.

Mom cringed and covered her eyes.

I covered my mouth with both hands so they wouldn't see me laughing.

Stripe headed out of the room, leaving Dweeble and my mom with the mess. I ran after him, following him all the way to the sliding glass door at the back of the house.

He gazed out at the yard, then looked up at me. "You have opposable thumbs," he seemed to be telling me. "So what are you waiting for?"

We both headed outside. The puppy sniffed the new tomato plants, while I checked out the rest of the yard. The entire space was enclosed within a wall of tan concrete bricks, stacked high over my head. I couldn't see the other backyards but I figured they all looked the same—mostly lawn with a small, cemented area by the door.

I sat down on the grass and leaned against the wall. Stripe took this as an invitation to come over and sniff me. Pretty soon he plopped down at my side. Since no one could see me, I stroked his coat. It felt so soft and silky I used both hands.

Mouth open, he panted. I guess the morning excitement wore him out.

The sun warmed my face. In the distance I saw rolling hills. Our old apartment had a view of the freeway, and we heard cars zoom past all day and night. I didn't mind it so much, but I wouldn't miss it, either. And okay, I'd never say so, but it felt nice having a real yard with grass and my own puppy.

When my mom came outside a minute later, I pulled my hand away and wrapped my arms around my knees, doing my best to look bored.

"There you are," she said, handing me a book. "We got you a dog-training manual to teach you how to take care of Stripe, or whatever you decide to name him."

"My gift comes with homework?" I asked.

"It's not homework. It'll be fun."

Easy for her to say.

The book was called *Good Dog! Raise Your Puppy Right*. The cover showed three fluffy baby Labradors lined up along a white picket fence—one yellow, one brown, and one black. None of them looked like Stripe. Of course, Stripe didn't look like any dog I'd ever seen. His large head seemed too big for his skinny body. And he wasn't exactly spotted, since there was black fur in his white spots and white fur mixed into his black parts. Especially on his back, where he had a huge black and white patch that was almost heart-shaped.

I flipped past the introduction and read the first page out loud.

> Before you even think about bringing your new puppy home, be sure to puppy-proof your house. If anything is in reach of your new puppy, you can bet that it'll be sniffed, tasted, chewed, or knocked over. You wouldn't believe how quickly a new puppy can do damage.

I looked up and said, "Guess you and Ted should have read this a couple of days ago, huh?"

Mom just smiled at me, kind of sadly. "I know this is hard for you, Annabelle. So many big changes to deal with, and you're being wonderful about it. I appreciate that. Please, though. Just give him a chance."

I stared down at the book, not answering her. I couldn't, because I didn't know if she was talking about the new puppy or about Dweeble.

chapter two
new friends with weird hats

"You were supposed to call me as soon as you got to your new house," Sophia said on the phone the next morning.

"I know, but yesterday was really busy. My mom and Dweeble got me a puppy."

"No fair!" Sophia cried. "I want a puppy!"

"He is pretty cute," I whispered. Sure, I was upstairs in my room, behind the closed door, but I needed to play it safe. I didn't want Mom and Dweeble to hear how happy I was about Stripe. If they knew I liked him, they'd think their plan worked. That's why I didn't pet him when I'd come downstairs for breakfast. I just ate my cornflakes silently and then took the portable phone upstairs so I could call my friends.

"When my dad moved out of our house, all I got was a cat," Sophia complained.

This was news to me. "When did you have a cat?"

Sophia sighed. "Three years ago. We only got to keep her for a few days because then my dad came home, and he's allergic."

"So what happened?"

"We gave her to my mom's cousin."

I wondered what would happen if things didn't work out with Mom and Dweeble. Who'd keep the puppy? Would we stay in this house, or move into another place? We couldn't go back to our old apartment because there were already other people living there. But maybe if we asked nicely, they'd let us have it back.

"So how's the house?" Sophia asked.

"It's okay," I said, even though it wasn't. When I woke up this morning I got scared because I didn't realize where I was at first. My old furniture looked small and shabby in my new room.

"Mia and I are meeting at the community pool. You should ask your mom to drive you over."

I groaned. "She won't do it. They're organizing their closets all morning."

"On the last day of summer?" asked Sophia.

"At least she's taking me to the mall later to get some school clothes."

"I'm so jealous. You don't have to wear a uniform anymore. *And* you get to go to school with boys."

Sophia has been obsessed with boys all summer and I don't get why. As far as I could tell, boys weren't so different from girls. Some were really nice and some were big jerks, and most were somewhere in between. And okay, this reasoning didn't exactly explain the whole camp dance disaster, but I figured that was a fluke thing. Like, maybe those boys had too much sugar that day, or perhaps it was due to the full moon.

I didn't bother trying to explain, though, because I knew Sophia would never understand.

When I heard my mom yelling from downstairs, I was actually glad I had an excuse to get off the phone.

"Um, I have to go," I said.

"Well, call me on Monday, after you get home from school, and don't forget this time."

"Okay."

I found Stripe and my mom at the bottom of the steps, playing tug-of-war with one of her sandals. She was on her knees, pulling at her shoe with both hands.

"Are you okay?" I asked.

"I'm fine, but my new sandal is a mess."

Since I didn't want her to get any ideas about giving the puppy back, I crouched down and called, "Hey, Stripe. Come here, boy."

The puppy was determined. His teeth stayed locked on the sandal and he jerked his head back and forth, trying to wrench it away from my mom.

"Here, Stripe," I tried, again.

"He doesn't know his name yet," said Mom. "I don't think so, anyway."

"Maybe he just doesn't *like* his name."

Mom pulled until the leather ripped, and then she let go with a gasp.

Unfazed, Stripe took the sandal into the living room, and we followed. Chasing after the dog was our new hobby, I guess.

He hid under the coffee table, guarding the shoe like it was the only food he'd seen all week. I crouched down and started crawling closer, but Mom said, "Let him have it. It's already ruined."

"You sure?" I asked, standing up.

"Positive. He'll get better once you start training him. I figured you could start right now, actually."

This was news to me. "I can?" I asked.

"Yes, unless you'd rather help unpack. It's your choice."

Some choice. I sighed an exaggerated sigh and said, "Fine."

Then I ran upstairs and got the book. It was pretty thick, which meant Stripe had a lot to learn. I sat down on my bed and started reading.

❧ UNDERSTANDING DOG-SPEAK ❧

Talk to dogs in their own language. Your tone is just as important as your words. *Stay? Sit? Come?* Don't ask them. Tell them. You're the boss, so act that way. Make your commands firm, short, and to the point. This is how you'll get dogs to listen to you.

"Stripe, no," I said in my normal voice. I had to admit, it didn't sound exactly strong or convincing.

"Stripe, no!" I repeated, louder this time, although maybe that was too loud. I didn't want him to think I was mad at him. I tried a few more times, until my mom poked her head in the room and asked me what was wrong.

"Nothing," I informed her.

"Then why were you yelling?"

"I'm just practicing my dog-speak." I held up the book to remind her. "You're the one who told me to do this, remember?"

"Oh, yes. Carry on." She answered me in her "British butler" voice. Mom and I both do that sometimes when we're alone. I'm not sure why.

❧ PACK YOUR TRAINING TOOLS ❧

Two facts: 1) Dogs love food. 2) Dogs never know where their next meal is coming from. Use these facts to your advantage. How so? Make food an incentive to get your dog to do what you want. It may feel like you're bribing your dog, but hey, who said there's anything wrong with bribery? Okay, maybe there is, but not when it comes to dog training. Yes, you love your dog. (We hope.) But you know what? Your dog is an animal. And it's your job to teach him or her how to behave around people.

So far these training tips seemed simple enough.

I flipped ahead to the chapter called "A Walk in the Park."

You weren't born knowing how to ride a bicycle. Well, guess what? Your dog wasn't born knowing how to walk on a leash.

According to the book, I had to get Stripe comfortable wearing the leash before I actually tried to walk him somewhere. I also needed to prove to him that walking with me was fun. This is where the bribery kicked in. If I called Stripe over, and praised him and gave him a treat once he came, he'd learn that listening to me was a good thing.

This all made sense. Figuring it was time to practice on a real dog, I closed the book and grabbed Stripe's leash. Then I pocketed a bunch of dog biscuits and went to find him. He was out back, digging up one of Mom's new tomato plants.

"Stop it!" I said, rushing over. "Hey, Stripe, cut it out! You can't do things like that! Mom's going to be mad."

My dog ignored me. Pretty soon I realized why. My voice was totally weak, and I used too many words.

"Stripe, no!" I spoke firmly this time. "Stop."

Now he looked up at me, tilting his head, like he was confused. Clearly he didn't understand what I was saying, but at least he seemed to know I was talking to him.

"Come," I said, figuring that was all it would take.

Stripe turned back to his hole and dug more furiously this time.

Oh, well. So much for that.

"Stop!" I called again. This time I pulled a biscuit out of my pocket, got closer, and waved it in front of his face. That sure got his attention.

Stripe's nose twitched as he sniffed at the biscuit with hungry eyes. Before he could take a bite, I walked backward.

Stripe watched the biscuit intently. Crouching low, he crept closer on mud-caked paws. I kept walking and Stripe kept following, more focused than ever.

I didn't stop moving until we were halfway across the lawn. "Good boy," I said, and fed him the biscuit, getting my fingers nice and slobbery in the process.

Stripe gulped it down and headed straight back to the plants.

Well, this was going to take some work. It's a good thing I didn't have anything better to do.

I called Stripe again. He looked up at me, but then decided that the plant was more interesting. Yes, my dog is more interested in a plant. Go me.

"Here, Stripe," I repeated, holding out another biscuit.

He came bounding over and jumped on me. Bracing myself, I stretched my arm over my head to keep it away from him. When he finally calmed down, I let him eat the treat.

Since he stood so close to me, I clipped the leash to his collar. He was so focused on the snack, he didn't even notice.

I led Stripe through the house to the front door. "Good boy," I told him, as we headed outside.

We walked up and down the cul-de-sac. It wasn't easy, because he stopped to sniff everything, and once he did notice he was on a leash he kept trying to get away from it. After a couple of trips, I sat down on the front lawn. Stripe plopped down next to me, resting his head on my leg. I guess all that training tired him out.

I put the leash around my wrist, just in case he got any ideas about running away. Not that I needed to. He stayed glued to my side like we were stuck together, courtesy of Elmer's.

Soon, a girl turned onto the street and zoomed by on a purple bicycle. She was tall and skinny, and she had on rainbow-striped leggings underneath a jeans skirt, with a white T-shirt on top. It was a hot day, but for some reason she wore a red ski cap over her curly brown hair.

She didn't look directly at me, but I could tell she noticed me, just by the way her head moved, ever so slightly, in my direction. When she got to the end of the cul-de-sac, she turned around and rode by again.

Finally, when she passed me a third time, I called out, "Hey there."

She kept riding like she didn't hear me. But when she rode past our neighbor's house she braked and planted her feet on the sidewalk. Looking over her shoulder she asked, "Did you say something?"

"I said hi," I replied.

She got off her bicycle and walked it over. "Oh. I thought you said, 'Hey there.'"

If she heard what I said the first time, I didn't know why she bothered asking. Still, I wasn't going to hold it against her. She was the first person to speak to me in the new neighborhood. (Mom and Dweeble didn't count.)

She set her bike down on the lawn and pointed to Stripe. "Is that your dog?"

I shrugged. "Sort of."

Stripe cocked his head and gazed at her. Maybe he wondered about her ski cap, too.

"What do you mean, sort of?"

"He's more like a consolation prize. My mom is trying to bribe me into liking it here."

"What's his name?"

"Right now I'm calling him Stripe, but only until I think of something better. I just got him last night."

"What grade are you in?" she asked.

"I'm going into sixth."

"At Birchwood?"

I nodded.

"Me, too." She pointed to the house across the street and said, "I live over there. Do you want to ride bikes or something?"

"I can't," I said. "I need to train the dog."

"Train him to do what?"

"Um, pretty much everything."

"Want some help?" she asked.

"Do you know anything about dogs?"

She shrugged. "I know I'm allergic, so I can't get too close, but I do have a hamster named Fuzzball."

Well, I figured that would have to do.

"I'm Annabelle."

"I'm Rachel."

"How come you're wearing that hat?"

"I don't want my hair to frizz on the first day of school," she said. "And my mom won't let me get it straightened until I turn thirteen, which is forever away."

"Oh," I said, since I didn't really know what that meant. I've heard of girls getting perms, but I didn't know what hair straightening was all about and I didn't want to ask. Maybe it was one of those things I was supposed to know already.

"Is your hair naturally blond?" Her questions were pointed like her features. She had a sharp nose and a sharp chin. "My cousin Liz gets highlights."

"It's always been like this," I said. "The color I mean. Sometimes I cut it shorter."

That was a dumb thing to say, but I didn't realize until it was too late.

Rachel didn't seem to care though, since she still sat down next to me on the grass and said, "My mom won't let me get highlights until I'm fifteen."

Stripe tried to sniff her but I held him back, because I didn't want her to sneeze or break out in hives or anything.

"So, where'd you move here from?" she asked.

"North Hollywood," I said. "It's about an hour away."

"I know. I've been there," Rachel said.

I had the feeling she was the type of girl who'd been lots of places, which was cool and kind of intimidating. Like when Sophia got to be in a focus group that tested the new Trident gum. She knew all about the improved packaging a whole year before it was available in stores. It doesn't sound like a big deal, but she talked about it so much it kind of became a big deal.

"I've lived on this street ever since I was born. I'm glad you're here now, because it's been pretty boring so far."

"My mom said there were tons of kids in this neighborhood."

Rachel plucked a single blade of grass and tied it into a knot. "There are some, but no one *good*. My friend Yumi lives ten blocks away, but that's kind of far, you know?"

I nodded, happy she thought I was good. At least I think that's what she meant. And no, she didn't know me yet. But obviously she thought I had potential.

"Hey, do you have your class schedule?" Rachel asked. "Because mine came in the mail last week."

"I think it's in the house, somewhere."

"Well, go get it and I'll get mine and meet you back here, okay?"

"Sure," I said. We both stood up. Stripe rolled onto his back and looked at me like he wanted a belly rub. "Let's go, buddy." I gave his leash a short tug. It took some coaxing but eventually I got him inside.

Mom couldn't find my schedule right away because our stuff was still only half unpacked. By the time I got back, Rachel was waiting for me, sitting cross-legged in the middle of our lawn. "Are you taking band?" she asked.

I looked down at my schedule, even though I knew I wasn't. "No. I'm in chorus."

"Oh, that's cool. Band kids are mostly nerdy, with the exception of the drummers, and I'm going to play the drums."

"Cool," I said, hoping that chorus wasn't nerdy as well. I wished I didn't care, but these things matter.

"I already bought the sticks and I've been practicing on the bottom of my hamper all summer," Rachel told me. "My mom wouldn't let me bring them outside now because she's afraid I'm going to lose them again. I'm already on my third pair."

"I sing in the shower sometimes."

It was supposed to be a joke—not a good one, I'll admit. But Rachel didn't take it that way. She tilted her head and blinked at me with her big brown eyes. "Really?" she asked.

"No," I said, shrugging. "But I like to sing." Our camp put on *Grease* this summer, and I got to play Sandy. I didn't tell Rachel because I didn't want to sound braggy. But I still kind of wished she knew.

We compared schedules. Turns out we had PE together, which met last period. And we had the same teacher for English, but my class met first and hers met right after lunch.

"That stinks," said Rachel. "I hardly have any classes with people I know. But you and I have lunch together. Want to eat with me and my friends? We're all meeting at my locker, right before."

"Okay," I said.

Just then someone called her name from across the street.

"That's my mom. I've got to go." Rachel stood up, so I did, too.

She climbed on to her bicycle. "I'll see you tomorrow, okay?"

"Wait, where's your locker?" I asked.

"It's number eleven-oh-seven," she said. "All the lockers are in one place, so you'll find it pretty easily."

"Um, what are you wearing?" I asked.

"Jeans," she said, like it wasn't a big deal. So I figured jeans were what I should wear, too.

I went inside and told my mom I was ready to go shopping. The mall was much smaller than the one in North Hollywood, but we still found some cool stores. I got two pairs of jeans, a pair of capri pants, some brown leather sandals, and a few T-shirts. My favorite one came pre-softened. It was light pink with three blue stars across the front, perfect for the first day of school. I hoped.

My stomach ached so much I hardly ate dinner,

even though we were having my favorite—macaroni and cheese. Mom and Dweeble had broccoli on the side, but she didn't make me eat any of it. Another bribe, probably, but I wasn't about to complain. Later that night, the grown-ups watched boring news in the living room on Dweeble's gigantic flat-screen television.

"Can Stripe sleep in my room tonight?" I asked.

Dweeble seemed surprised. "I thought you didn't like Stripe."

"Well, I don't, but it still doesn't seem fair, making him sleep in a cage."

"It's a kennel, not a cage," Mom said.

"It has steel bars and a lock," I pointed out.

"He doesn't mind it," said Dweeble. "Puppies feel more comfortable in confined spaces."

"Did he tell you that?" I asked.

"No, but the dog-training book did," said Mom.

"I guess I missed that chapter."

"It's for his own safety," said Dweeble. "Imagine if he opened up the cabinet under the sink and drank the cleaning supplies. He'd be poisoned."

"There aren't any cleaning supplies in my bed-room. Just a bunch of boxes filled with clothes and books."

Mom looked at Dweeble, and I don't know why. I was *her* daughter and Stripe was supposed to be *my* puppy.

Before I reminded her of this, she turned back to me and said, "If you want, we can move the kennel into your room, as long as you promise to put Stripe inside when you go to bed."

"Cool," I said. "I will."

So at the next commercial they set everything up. Dweeble carried the kennel upstairs, and Mom laid a towel down underneath, so it wouldn't mess up the new carpet. I made sure they were careful not to step on my first-day-of-school outfit, which I'd laid out in the middle of the floor.

When they finally left us alone, I found an old tennis ball and Stripe and I played a game that was sort of like fetch. Basically, I rolled the ball across the room, and Stripe ran after it, caught it, and started gnawing on it. Then I pried it out of his mouth so we could start all over again. It was way more fun than it sounds.

Soon Mom came in and said I should get to bed. It wasn't easy putting Stripe back in the kennel. He struggled and nipped at my hands with his sharp little puppy fangs. He seemed to be telling me he wasn't near ready for sleep. And in case I didn't get the message the first time, once we did manage to close the grated door behind him, he started whimpering.

Mom frowned at the cage. "I hope he doesn't keep you up."

"It'll be fine," I said, as I climbed into bed.

"You'll be better than fine, Annabelle. You'll love your new school. I can feel it."

"Mom!" I yelled, since she was being insane. Usually she's a fairly cool mom, and she understands the important stuff. But then every once in a while, she'll make some crazy remark like this.

"I will not love Birchwood. It's still school, you know."

"You're right. Sorry, honey. Good night." She kissed my forehead.

"Good night." I pulled the covers up to my chin and rolled onto my side.

Soon after my mom left, Stripe began crying in sad, squeaky bursts of noise. He didn't keep me up, though. I was up anyway. My mind raced. Starting tomorrow, I'd have six different teachers instead of one. This would be the first time I'd be at school without a uniform. I liked the new jeans and pink T-shirt I planned to wear just fine, but what if they were the wrong kind? Or what if Rachel made a mistake and no one else wore jeans on the first day of school? And speaking of Rachel, what if I couldn't find her at lunchtime? What if she thought I didn't want to eat with her? How insulting would that be? She'd get mad and maybe she'd turn her friends against me. My first potential enemies, and school hadn't even started.

I rolled onto my back and stared at the ceiling. Then I rolled to the side. My pillow got too hot so I flipped it over, but nothing helped. I looked at my desk. It used to sit next to my bed, so it could double as a nightstand. Now it was clear across the room, five big steps away. My alarm clock still rested on the edge, forcing me to squint to see the glowing green numbers. Eleven thirty, it read. I only ever stayed up that late when Sophia and Mia slept over.

I couldn't believe I had to go to school without them.

Stripe kept crying and it wasn't right. Dweeble had said he was in the cage for his own safety, but there wasn't anything dangerous in my bedroom. Plus, maybe he was missing his old home, like I was missing mine. The least I could do was let him walk around a bit, stretch his little legs.

I got out of bed and tiptoed over. Stripe thumped his tail hard and fast against the newspaper lining the bottom of the cage.

"Shhh," I whispered. "You have to promise to be good, okay?"

As soon as I set Stripe free he jumped up and licked my face.

"Down, boy," I said, trying not to giggle too hard. "It's okay."

I set one of my pillows down on the floor and motioned him over. After sniffing around a bit, Stripe lay down on it.

"Good boy." I stroked his fur. "Now let's go to sleep."

I figured I'd wake up early and put Stripe back in his cage before my mom came in, so she'd never know he didn't sleep in there for the whole night. That was the plan, anyway.

Stripe fell asleep pretty fast, and I guess I finally did, too.

The next thing I knew, I woke up to my mom gasping, "Annabelle, what happened?"

I opened my eyes. The bright sun blazed through my window, casting light on the disaster area formerly known as my bedroom.

Pages from my loose-leaf notebook lay scattered across the floor. Some were wrinkled and others were torn up. My clothes were in a pile by the door. Mom held up my pink T-shirt and stared at me through the raggedy hole in its center.

Leaping out of bed, I reached for my new jeans. The cuff on one leg was missing, and the other cuff was frayed and slimy with slobber.

I turned to Stripe, who sat in the corner looking innocent. He had a strange chew toy in his mouth. Also known as one of my new sandals.

Stripe had ruined my entire first-day-of-school outfit, and he wagged his tail happily, like he'd done me some big huge favor.

"What am I going to wear?" I cried.

"Don't know but you'd better decide fast," Mom said. "We all overslept. If we're not out the door in fifteen minutes, you'll be late for school."

chapter three
the bad beginning

We must've lost power in the middle of the night," Mom said as we sped toward campus. "It's a good thing Ted woke up, or we might all still be asleep."

I wasn't about to thank Dweeble for anything. If it weren't for him, we'd be in our old apartment—where our alarm clocks had never let us down. But instead, I had to show up to my new school looking like a total slob. There hadn't been time to do anything but shower and throw on the first thing I could find. That's why I was wearing a green T-shirt and a gray plaid skirt, which had been part of my old uniform from St. Catherine's. I didn't even dry my hair. I had to pull it into a damp ponytail without combing through all the bumps.

This day was already a disaster and I hadn't even set foot on campus. My heart thumped at about a million beats a minute as my mom pulled up to Birchwood Middle School.

"I'll be right here at three thirty," she said. "Have a wonderful first day."

There she goes again with her crazy talk.

"Okay, thanks. Bye." I got out of the car, shouldered my backpack, and ran. My ponytail slipped, but there wasn't time to fix it. As the late bell chimed, kids streamed into their classrooms. Meanwhile, I still had to find mine.

I tore across the quad in search of Room 604, where I had English. When I found Room 603, I began to relax. There was just one problem. Room 605 was right next to it, and Room 601 was on the other side. Room 604 was nowhere in sight. Suddenly the halls were empty. Everyone else was where they were supposed to be. And me? I was alone, with no idea where to go.

I stared from my wrinkled schedule to the doors in front of me, as if the missing room would appear magically, if only I wished for it hard enough.

My stomach ached. Before I knew it, tears welled up in my eyes.

Stupid Birchwood. At St. Catherine's, everything was in one tall building. Room Nine came after Room Eight, which came after Room Seven, and there was no skipping around or missing numbers.

I circled the whole quad and then stopped in front of Room 603, again. I didn't know what else to do.

"Hey!" someone said from behind me.

I turned around. Standing in front of me was a kid with spiky blond hair and brown eyes. He was a head taller than me, and he seemed pretty grown up. Like he could have been an eighth grader, even. I couldn't figure out what to say. So I kept quiet, which probably made me look dumb.

"You lost?" he asked.

"Nope." I hardly ever lied, but at the moment, it seemed like a good idea.

The guy smirked. "Sure you are."

I took a step away.

"You're a sixth grader, right?" he asked.

So it was that obvious. "Yup." I nodded.

He held out his hand. At first I thought he wanted to shake, so I held out my empty hand, too. But he just laughed and said, "No, let's see your schedule."

I handed it over. I didn't want to, but couldn't just refuse. He already thought I was weird enough.

"Room six-oh-four isn't here," I said. This was clear, but I felt like I needed to fill the silence.

"No kidding." He looked at the classrooms in front of me and grinned. Then he handed back my schedule and said, "So you don't know about the fire, huh?"

"Fire?"

"Room six-oh-four burned down last spring. It doesn't exist."

"Then why does my schedule say I'm supposed to go there?" I asked.

"Computer glitch. There was an announcement about it this morning. Didn't you hear?"

I shook my head no.

The guy nodded. "Yes, they said that everyone with Room six-oh-four printed on their schedule should report to Room six-oh-five, instead."

"Really?" I asked. "You're sure?"

"Positive. Stuff like that happens all the time around here. You'll see."

This seemed kind of weird, but I *did* miss the morning announcements, I guess. I wanted to ask him one more time, but he'd already walked away. His walk wasn't normal, though. He moved his feet in a slightly bouncy way and puffed out his chest. His shoulders swayed, like he was listening to music.

After the guy turned the corner, I took a deep breath, retied my ponytail, and opened the door to Room 605.

"Sorry I'm late," I said, slinking my way inside. The teacher smiled and nodded to the only free seat. It was in the front row at the other end of the room.

I sat down quickly, opened my backpack, and pulled a freshly sharpened pencil from the lucky case Mia gave me back when she found out I had to move. It felt good, finally being where I was supposed to be. Maybe Birchwood wouldn't be so bad. At least, that's what I was thinking before I looked at the board and almost had a heart attack. The words swam before me, incomprehensible. Even worse, the teacher was speaking to me and I'd no idea what she was saying.

"¿Cuál es su nombre y de donde es usted?"

"What?" I asked, my voice plagued with panic.

The girl to my left giggled behind her hand. The guy behind me didn't even try to hide his laughter. He just let it out.

I slowly turned around and surveyed the strange faces. Something wasn't right. These kids looked too old to be in the sixth grade.

"What's your name and where are you from?" the teacher asked.

At least I understood the question this time.

"My name is Annabelle and I'm from North Hollywood."

"Hablas en espanol, por favor."

"Um, what?" I asked.

"Answer in Spanish," she said.

"But I can't." I stared down at my desk. Someone had carved "I 'heart' Dave" into the wood. "I don't speak Spanish."

"Then how on earth did you get into Spanish III?"

Uh-oh. "I thought this was sixth grade English," I whispered.

Now the entire class laughed.

"Settle down," the teacher told them as she walked over to my desk. "Let me see your schedule, please."

I handed it over.

She read it, frowned, then turned to her students. "Please write a five-paragraph essay, describing how you spent your summer vacation."

As the class groaned, she motioned for me to follow

her outside. I gathered my things as quickly as I could, not even taking the time to put my pencil back in its case. (What would be the point? Clearly all the luck had worn off.)

Once we were in the hall, the teacher asked, "Do you know about the numbering system for the two quads here?"

"There's a system?" I asked, as I bit back tears.

She pointed to the first line of my schedule. "See that E? That stands for East, as in East Quad. You're in the West Quad now. The rooms in the East Quad buildings have even numbers. The rooms in the West Quad buildings have odd numbers. That's why there's no Room six-oh-four over here."

I wanted to apologize but I had to hold my breath to keep from crying.

It was nice of her to be so understanding, but also kind of annoying, because it seemed like she felt sorry for me.

"Don't be upset. This happens every year. They really should change it. Although if you can remember that 'E' stands for both East and even, it'll be easier." She pointed toward the other quad. "Just go past the lockers and turn right. Room six-oh-four is the third door in."

"Okay. Thank you," I managed to squeak out, before hurrying off.

Once I made it to the right place, I burst through the door to find an entire roomful of eyes staring at me.

"Can I help you?" asked the teacher, a short man

with thick gray hair, black chunky-framed glasses, and a big belly hanging over his belt.

"Sorry I'm late. I got lost. I . . . well . . . this is my first day."

"Yes, this is everyone's first day," he said.

"Right. Of course." I scanned the room, happy to find an empty desk in the back corner. I made my way toward it.

"Not so fast," he said, pointing to a desk in the front row. "Why don't you sit over there, and tell us your name."

I sank into the chair. "I'm Annabelle Stevens."

"Hello, Annabelle. I'm Mr. Beller." He looked down at his roster and frowned. "Well, this is strange. I don't see an Annabelle Stevens in this class."

"You don't?" I stood up fast—not realizing my backpack was still in my lap. It tumbled to the floor.

"Kidding," he said, and the entire class laughed.

Wow. Looks like Dweeble's got some competition in the "worst sense of humor, ever" category.

I sat back down and picked up my bag, wishing I'd just stayed in Spanish III. No, I didn't speak the language, but at least that teacher had been nice to me.

Mr. Beller didn't make any more jokes at my expense, but I still didn't like him. He made everyone sign a contract that read, "This year, I [insert your name] promise to work hard and always give it my all."

It seemed pointless, since everyone plans on giving

school "their all" on the first day of the new year. It's easy to do then, before the work piles on.

That's what I was thinking when I felt something hard thump against my back. It pushed my whole body forward. It happened again, and then a third time. Someone was kicking the back of my chair.

When I turned around, the guy behind me pretended he was writing in his notebook. His shaggy, dark bangs hung down over the tops of his glasses. I stared at him for a few seconds, but he wouldn't look up. I could tell he noticed, though. As soon as I faced forward, he kicked me again.

I tried to ignore him, but it was hard. He kicked my chair all through class, and I don't know why I didn't tell him to stop. When Margaret Sinclair pulled my hair in the third grade, I'd had no problem telling her to cut it out. Yet now, I just sat there and took the kicks.

Class finally ended, and luckily, I had social studies in Room 606, right next door.

Unfortunately, as soon as I walked into the room, some guy got up and said, "I'm Spamabelle Stevens and this is my first day!" His voice was higher pitched than SpongeBob sucking on a helium balloon. I don't sound like that at all. Still, all his friends laughed and gave each other high fives. It wasn't even that funny. But the way they carried on, you'd think it was the best joke they'd heard all year. And okay, the school year was only a few hours old, but this didn't make me feel any better.

When I got to French class, some skinny red-haired guy called out, "Hi, Spamabelle."

My first day of junior high, and I was already a total joke! I wondered if Ted's dweebiness was contagious. Maybe it spread through the walls of our house, like mold or termites.

At least I didn't run into the guy with spiky blond hair from this morning. That would've been the worst.

When the bell rang, releasing me from French, I raced to my locker.

After dumping my new books inside, I found Rachel. She was leaning against her locker, looking normal and totally happy in a light blue v-neck T-shirt, faded jeans, and flip-flops. Her fingers and toenails were painted pink. She'd left the ski cap at home and her hair frizzed only slightly.

"Hey," she said.

"Hi, are you ready?" I hoped she hadn't changed her mind about letting me eat with her. What if word already got out that I was a total spaz who crashed other people's classes?

"Of course. I'm starving. Yumi is saving us space over in the West Quad. That's where all the sixth graders eat."

I wondered how she knew that, and wished I could ask. Instead, I followed her down the hall, silently.

"So, what do you think so far?" she asked.

I considered lying and saying everything was completely fabulous—the best morning of my life—but in the end, I told her about our alarm clocks and how Stripe chewed up my clothes. "That's why I look like a slob."

"I like your skirt. It's cute."

Rachel probably only said that to be nice, but I decided to believe her. It was the first good thing to happen to me all day.

That, and lunch. We walked to a big outdoor seating area, and wove through crowded picnic tables until we found her friends, Emma, Claire, and Yumi, who'd saved us seats.

When we got there, Emma was in the middle of unpacking her lunch. She lined up her food in a neat row and ate everything in order—a bite of turkey sandwich, a sip of lemonade, a carrot stick, then a bite of oatmeal cookie. Then she went back to the beginning. She looked tan, and had thick, dark hair with a perfect part in the middle. Her white T-shirt had pink trim and her pink socks were trimmed in white, which matched her pink and white plaid shorts, which all seemed to match her personality—quiet and orderly.

Yumi was wearing a Dodgers cap, and she ate like a regular person. She also showed us pictures of her baby sister, Suki, from a pink Hello Kitty photo album. Yumi explained that Suki was only three months old and that's why she had no hair. I looked at all the pictures to be polite, even though they all seemed the same: sleeping baby—sometimes in yellow footy pajamas, and sometimes in blue and white striped footy pajamas.

"This one is my favorite." Yumi pointed to a picture of the baby wearing a baseball uniform. "Isn't she cute?"

"Yup, but I already saw it, I think."

"No, she was wearing the Dodgers' *away* uniform in the other one. This is their home uniform. Plus, in this one she has on socks that look like cleats."

"Yumi is obsessed with the Dodgers," Rachel explained. "But you probably figured that out already."

"I'm not obsessed. I just think they're the greatest team that ever was and I never miss a game."

"Exactly," said Rachel.

"My dad and I have season tickets. He moved here from Japan to play baseball at UCLA, and almost got recruited to a minor league team in Sacramento," Yumi told me. "Do you like baseball?"

"I guess," I said. "But I'm more into basketball."

"So are you a Lakers fan?"

"Um, I mean I like playing basketball. I don't watch games on TV or anything."

Just then Claire came over with a giant taco salad from the cafeteria. As soon as she sat down, she told me she recognized me from English class. I'm surprised I didn't remember Claire, since she didn't look like the other sixth graders. She was much taller than the rest of us, and had long, curly red hair pulled back with a wide blue headband, which matched her blue eyes. She wore a tie-dye shirt and a faded jeans skirt with frayed edges.

Of course, if we had English together, that meant she'd witnessed my humiliation. "That was so embarrassing," I said.

She shook her head. "Don't worry. No one cares if you're late on the first day."

"Mr. Beller sure cared."

"Well, no one likes him. My sister had him two years ago and she said he's way strict, and just, not nice."

I was about to ask Claire about her other classes, but I never got the chance to, because just then a shadow loomed over our table.

Everyone got really quiet, except for Rachel. She glanced up and made a face, asking, "What do you want, Jackson?"

I looked up and almost choked on my chicken salad. Towering over us was the guy who'd told me to walk into Spanish III. I quickly turned my head away and hunched over my sandwich, hoping he didn't notice me.

Last year in science we studied spiders that change color to hide from their predators. More than anything, I wished I could do the same thing. At least my shirt was green, so I blended in with the nearby grass. Okay, that's a stretch. But I wished it were true.

Luckily, he only spoke to Rachel. "Don't be late," he said. "I've got Tae Kwon Do after school."

"I won't be late," she replied, annoyed. "I'm never late."

"Well, don't start today," he said.

My foot tingled with pins and needles but I was too scared to shake it awake. I couldn't even move. If he and Rachel carpooled together, that probably meant he lived near Clemson Court. Could my luck get any worse?

"Hey, I know you!" he said, pointing at me.

Great. That's just perfect. I shook my head, silently pleading with him not to tell everyone how he'd tricked me.

Rachel said, "This is Annabelle. She lives on our street."

Our street? Clemson Court wasn't that big.

"That's cool," he said, smiling in this obviously fake-nice way. "Let me know if you need any help, okay? This place can be kind of confusing sometimes."

I felt my face get redder and redder as I looked down at my half-eaten sandwich. Suddenly I'd lost my appetite.

"Give us some privacy, will you?" said Rachel.

"Whatever. I'm outta here."

When Jackson finally turned to go, I realized why his walk was so distinct. He moved like he knew people were watching him. Like he knew he was cool.

Once I was sure he was out of earshot, I asked, "Wait, you *know* that guy?"

Rachel scrunched her nose up, like she'd just smelled something rotten. Yumi and Claire leaned their heads together and giggled. Emma just shook her head.

"What's so funny?" I asked, worried.

"Of course I know him," said Rachel. "He's my brother."

chapter four
the loner table

Instead of getting my own desk in science, I had to share a table with two other students. Or, I should say, I was supposed to share a table. But that would require actually knowing someone who wanted to sit with me.

Since I didn't, I quickly headed to the last empty table and sat in the middle chair so it wouldn't look too empty. Then I watched everyone else group off. Each new kid headed into class and scanned the room until he or she saw someone they knew. Some asked for permission to sit. Others just sat, like it was understood. These were their friends, so it made perfect sense. Where else would they sit?

Finally, one boy walked over to my table and asked, "Is this seat taken?"

"Nope," I said, relieved that someone would finally choose to sit next to me.

But instead, he picked up the chair and carried it to a table in the back row.

I snuck a peek behind me and saw him join a

table that already had three boys. One I recognized from English: the kicker.

Soon another boy came over and took the chair to my left, without asking permission this time. So now there were five boys squished around the table behind me and I was stuck by myself.

I wondered if maybe these boys were friends with Jackson, who'd told them how he'd tricked me. Or maybe they could just tell I was the biggest nerd in school.

When Stripe peed on the rug last night, Mom and Dweeble used a special cleanser to wipe it up, because dogs have a highly developed sense of smell. My mom explained that if Stripe detected any trace of his pee on the rug, he'd go in the same spot again and make that place his bathroom.

Maybe boys were like Stripe, and I was carrying around some sort of "nerd scent" that only they could sniff out.

Yes, I knew this was unlikely, but how else could I explain it?

After the final bell rang the teacher got up from her desk and called the class to attention. Her name was Ms. Roberts and she was kind of fat, and I don't mean that in a mean way—just, that's the first thing I noticed about her. Her hair was long and pulled back in a low ponytail. When she called the class to attention, she sang her words in a pretty-sounding voice.

After roll call, she passed out a packet that outlined

the different units we'd be studying this year. "But before we go over it I'm going to pass around a seating chart," she said. "We'll need to split up the class into eight lab groups of three people each."

I looked around the room. All the other groups were split naturally. My empty table and the overly full table behind me were the only ones that were messed up. And suddenly everyone noticed.

I heard whispers. Giggles, too. It was like Spanish III all over again, except now there was no escape. I sat up straight and kept my eyes on Ms. Roberts.

"Which two of you are going to join Annabelle?" she asked the guys behind me.

I didn't turn around but sensed they were all frozen in their seats.

"You." Ms. Roberts pointed.

No one acknowledged her, as far as I could tell.

She sighed, impatiently. "The young man with the glasses. Don't pretend like you don't hear me. That won't work here. Now, what's your name?"

"Me?" asked a guy with a high-pitched voice.

"Yes, you. What's your name?"

"Tobias Miller," he mumbled.

"Please move to the table in front of you, Mr. Miller."

"That's not fair. I was here first." He sounded plenty whiny.

"Trust me. You don't want me to ask twice," said Ms. Roberts, all business.

I heard a notebook slamming and then a chair

scraping against the floor as Tobias dragged his seat over next to mine. Great—the kicker from first period.

"You, too," she said to someone else, who immediately groaned, like he had some horrible stomach flu.

Somehow, sitting with me had turned into a punishment. My face burned red with humiliation.

Before I knew it, there was a boy on either side of me. Besides the shaggy hair, glasses, and annoying feet, Tobias had thick eyebrows and kind of a big nose.

The other guy, Oliver, had short dark hair, tan skin, and green eyes. He wore baggy shorts and a T-shirt with some surf logo across the front. If Sophia and Mia were here, they'd get all giggly because he's so cute. They'd think so, anyway. Me? I could already tell he was too mean to like.

"What are you staring at?" he asked, moving his stuff to the edge of the table, so that he was as far from me as possible.

"Nothing," I said.

"Thanks a lot, Spamabelle," Tobias grumbled to me, as if it was my fault for existing.

"Spamabelle?" asked Oliver.

"That's her name," said Tobias.

They talked over me like I wasn't even there.

Girls at St. Catherine's were never this mean. Not on the first day of school, at least. You had to do something wrong first, like try to copy off someone on a test, or spill grape juice down the front of your shirt, or accidentally tuck the bottom of your skirt into your underwear after a trip to the bathroom. These guys were being mean to me for simply occupying the same space. It's not like I wanted to share a table with them, either. But I didn't say so. I didn't say anything.

The girl at the table in front of us passed the seating chart back. I wrote my name in the middle space of the Table Number Seven box, cementing my place in a very bad situation.

When I passed the chart to Tobias, he asked to borrow my pen, although not in a particularly nice way.

"Um, can I have that?" he asked, pointing.

I handed it over. After writing his name down, he handed the chart to Oliver, keeping my pen. It's not like I cared. I had six more in my backpack. It was just, well, how could Tobias act like a jerk and take my pen? And not even thank me for it, or anything?

Why doesn't he have his own pen, anyway? Who doesn't bring a pen on the first day of school? I reached into my backpack for a second one.

Then I tried to pay attention as Ms. Roberts showed us some of the equipment we'd be using this year. She held up shiny silver microscopes, glass petri dishes, and fragile-looking test tubes. She told us how careful we'd have to be, because the stuff was dangerous. Also, the PTA sprung for new supplies three years ago and they were supposed to last for another six.

By the time the bell rang, Tobias still hadn't returned my pen. I tried not to care, but he was a mean chair-kicker who called me names for no reason. He didn't deserve my pen.

The rest of the day was fine, in that no one teased me and I didn't get too lost. Still, I was relieved to finally spot my mom's car among the sea of traffic in the parking lot. As soon as I got in she hugged me. I was glad to see her, too, but wiggled out of her grasp, because people might see.

"Mom, stop." I looked out the window. No one was laughing, or even looking, but you can never be too careful.

"I can't help it," she said. "You're just so grown up and I'm so proud of you."

"For starting sixth grade, like a billion other kids?"

"Yes."

After passing the line of school buses, we drove by Rachel and Jackson.

"Oh look, there's your friend!" My mom waved.

I ducked down in my seat and yelled, "Cut it out!"

"What's wrong?" she asked.

"Nothing," I said, since the real problem was too hard to explain. Rachel stood next to Jackson, who swung his backpack around and around over his head. Kids had to make a circle around him so they wouldn't get hit. If someone wasn't paying attention and walked too close, they'd get clocked in the face, for sure. I'd only known Jackson since this morning, but something told me this was typical behavior.

"Who's that cute boy with Rachel?"

"Mom!"

I didn't want to say hi to Rachel in front of Jackson, because if they saw me, maybe they'd get to talking and Jackson would tell her about the mean trick he'd pulled. Maybe Rachel would think I was dumb for falling for it. Maybe she'd tell her friends and they wouldn't let me hang out with them at lunch. Then who would I eat with tomorrow? My lab partners from science? I think not.

chapter five
stripe gets trained. sort of.

As soon as we got home, I ran to Stripe's kennel, which someone had set up in the living room. When I let him out, Stripe jumped up and tried to lick my face. I bent down, so he could reach. It's not that I wanted my face to get slobbered on. It's just, well, he was too cute not to pet.

His whole body wiggled, and he raced back and forth from me to the door. It looked like he wanted to go out and he wanted to say hi, but he couldn't figure out which thing he wanted to do first.

Before long, I forgot all about my lousy school day. I didn't even care that we lived far from my old friends, and across the street from some jerk. Dweeble was still at work and would be for a while. Until then, it was just me, my mom, and my dog.

Standing up, I headed to the sliding glass door so I could let him out. But before I made it, he peed all over the floor, which wasn't cute at all.

"Hey, Mom?" I called.

"Yes," she asked, coming into the room.

"Stripe just peed inside again." I pointed to the mess on the floor.

"Oh, dear," she said. "Well, I'll clean it up this time, but will you take him outside and do some training work?"

"Let's go, Stripe." I opened up the back door and let him out. Then I went upstairs to get the puppy-training book. I figured I had to get Stripe trained pretty quickly. If he peed in the house too many more times, my mom might start asking me to clean up after him. Or even worse, she might want to get rid of him.

I brought the book into the den. It was my favorite room in the new house, mostly because it reminded me of our old apartment.

All our same comfy furniture was set up in there. If I could ignore the barf green wall-to-wall carpet, and just focus on the familiar tan easy chairs and the red ceramic lamps on the wooden side tables, I could pretend like I was back at home in North Hollywood. It even smelled kind of like our old place. Or at least, the leather from the easy chairs smelled the same. I climbed into my favorite one, kicked off my shoes, and started reading.

Training Stripe wasn't going to be easy. There were so many things I needed to teach him. He had to stop chewing up our stuff and stop peeing inside. It would also be cool if he'd sit and stay on command, not to mention come when I called him. And those were just the basics.

I read a chapter titled "Sit!," which was self-explanatory. Then I skipped ahead to the section called, *You Can't Go Wrong with Positive Reinforcement*. Basically, it talked about how when your dog does something good, you have to let him know it with lots of praise and enthusiasm.

Then I brought the book outside so we could practice.

I got Stripe to sit by lightly pressing down on his back with my right hand, while raising my left hand up and over his head. As his eyes followed my left hand, his head moved back and he sat down. "Sit," I said, so he'd learn the word. "Good sit."

I kept my voice firm and my commands short. Amazingly, Stripe responded to what I said, which made me want to teach him more stuff. And the more I taught him, the easier it was.

Of course, everything seemed easy with Stripe. All I had to do was read the dog-training book, where the rules were spelled out. Learn the rules, teach your dog the rules, and bam—you have an obedient dog. Presto. Simple. Change-O.

I just wish there were lessons like that for how to survive middle school. Not that my day was all bad. Lunch was fun until Jackson showed up. PE went well. Of course, I just hung around with Rachel the whole time. And no one made fun of me in chorus—maybe because there were about thirty girls in the class and only four boys.

That's when I realized it. I had no trouble, as long

as I was surrounded by girls. So what I really needed was a book that taught me how to deal with boys. If only there was such a thing.

After Stripe and I got bored with the training, I went inside for a snack. I was surprised to see my mom peeling carrots over the kitchen sink.

"Good day, Mum. Isn't it too early to eat?" I used my fake British accent, even though it wasn't nearly as good as hers.

"It's almost six," she told me in her regular voice.

"Hi, Annabelle. How's the puppy training going?" Dweeble asked.

I jumped at the sound of his voice. I didn't even know he was home, but there he stood—leaning in the doorframe between the kitchen and dining room. He wore running clothes. Baggy orange shorts that were so bright they hurt my eyes, and an old green T-shirt. He reminded me of an Oompa Loompa from Willy Wonka's chocolate factory. A stretched-out, giant Oompa Loompa—one that got caught in the taffy machine, I guess.

"I didn't know you were here," I said, embarrassed to be caught acting British in front of Dweeble. It was my and Mom's thing. No one else knew about it.

"Things were slow at the office, so I thought I'd cut out early and squeeze in a run before dinner."

"Huh," I said, just to say something, since no one else did.

"I hear you've been doing a great job with Stripe's training," Dweeble said.

"That's not his permanent name, you know."

"Oh, I know." Dweeble replied. "And I'm sure you'll come up with something better soon. Any ideas, yet?"

I shook my head. "Nope. I'm still thinking."

I didn't want him to be so nice. I just wanted him to go away, but he kept on talking.

"The thing is, and you probably know this, you should come up with a new name for him before he gets used to the old one. Because the later you give him a different name, the harder it'll be to make it stick."

Actually, I didn't know that, but it made sense.

I glanced at my mom, who'd moved on to peeling a cucumber. If she started calling me Gertrude all of a sudden, I wouldn't exactly come running. And not just because Gertrude is a weird name. Of course, if my name was Gertrude, I'd make everyone call me Gertie, which is kind of cool.

"Did you have a good day?" asked Dweeble. "What do you think of Birchwood?"

Ugh! I'd almost forgotten about my rotten first day. Figured Dweeble would have to go and remind me.

"How was *your* day?" I asked, just so he'd cut it out with the third degree.

Dweeble blinked—happy and surprised that I asked. "It was very nice, actually. I had a productive meeting with a client. And like I said before, it was relatively quiet, so I got to come home early."

I'd no idea what he was talking about, but nodded

anyway. Dweeble was an accountant at a firm that sold insurance. Or maybe he sold insurance to accountants. Mom told me once but I hadn't been paying attention and now it was too late to ask. I wondered how many slow days he had. Was he going to come home early all the time? I wanted to ask, but I'm not *that* rude.

"Cool," I said instead, because I had to say something.

Then I glanced at Mom, who smiled up at Dweeble. It gave me the strangest pangs in my belly.

She really liked this guy. It didn't matter that the kitchen was yellow, or that our new dog was out of control. Nor did she care that I had a lousy first day at Birchwood. Okay, true, she didn't know my first day was so bad. But maybe I didn't tell her because I didn't want to mess up her great new life.

"Well, I'd better head out," said Dweeble, winking at my mom.

I don't understand winking. I mean, unless you've got something stuck in your eye, what's the point?

Once he was gone, my mom dumped the cucumber slices into some weird blue bowl I'd never seen before. Our wooden salad bowl sat nearby, in the center of the counter. Now it was filled with peaches and plums and some fat red grapes. I don't know why but it made me want to cry.

"What's wrong?" Mom asked, when she caught me staring.

"Your salad bowl."

"I thought it looked nice out on the counter." She

rotated the bowl a quarter of a turn and beamed at it, like everything was so very perfect.

"But it's not a fruit bowl."

"You don't always have to be so literal, Annabelle."

I know it was just a bowl, but at the same time, it wasn't just a bowl. Staring at the thing, so chock full of fruit, it made me feel empty inside. "You think everything is a nice change, but you could have at least kept this one thing."

Mom put down her knife and wiped her hands on a dish towel. "Come show me what you've been teaching the dog, honey."

As we headed out, she put her arm around my shoulders, like she was trying to tell me everything was okay, but it wasn't. And I don't even mean the living with Dweeble part.

We walked out the sliding glass door, straight into a brand-new disaster.

Stripe was digging up Mom's vegetable garden. He'd already destroyed one tomato plant and was now working on his second.

Mom ran over and tried to shoo Stripe out of the way, but he wasn't giving up so easily.

"Oh, Stripe, how could you do this?" She grabbed his collar and pulled him from the mess. Except he didn't let go of the stalk so it snapped off and three green tomatoes dropped to the ground. Mom picked up a tomato and held it up to Stripe asking, "Do you know how much time and effort and money I spent on this?"

Um, Stripe had no idea. Mom seemed too upset, so I figured it wasn't a good time to teach her about *Dog-Speak* or *Positive Reinforcement*.

Instead, we put Stripe in the kennel and I helped her finish preparing dinner.

When she thought I wasn't looking, she dumped the fruit into a different bowl and put the salad in the old one. But by then, I didn't care.

As I put plates around the table, I wondered if we'd have to eat like this every night: with a table-cloth and folded napkins and vegetables.

When it was just me and Mom, we usually ate at the kitchen counter, or sometimes even on the coffee table in front of the TV. Whenever she was too tired to cook, which was most of the time, we either got Chinese food delivered, or we picked up chicken and ribs from this really good barbecue place.

Today was Monday, my third night in Westlake, and we hadn't eaten takeout once.

Anyway, our old coffee table was gone. Mom sold it on Craigslist because we didn't need two. And yesterday, when I put my soda can down on Dweeble's coffee table, he rushed over with a coaster. "Here, you should always use one of these," he'd said. "This table was imported from France."

He'd been really nice about it but it was still annoying. What's the point of having a coffee table if you can't eat off it? That's the whole reason they were invented.

"Do you have homework?" Mom asked, poking her head into the dining room.

I set the last plate down on the table. "On the first day of school? Are you kidding?"

"You're going to get a lot of work at Birchwood, Annabelle. Just wait. Sixth grade is hard."

Well, I knew that was true. But the hard part had nothing to do with what the teachers dished out.

chapter six
rude wake-ups (and other not-fun facts about birchwood middle school)

Mom drank coffee to help her wake up every morning. Dweeble liked caffeinated tea with honey. My new wake-up call? A heavy dose of being kicked in the back over and over and over again, all through first period.

Bright and early on Tuesday morning, Mr. Beller tried to explain the difference between a metaphor and a simile. At my old school I'd have been yawning until lunch. Not here. Every time the teacher turned around to write something on the white board, Tobias kicked me.

I figured he'd leave me alone if I ignored him long enough.

I figured wrong.

Halfway through class, I switched tactics and attempted to skooch my chair out of kicking range. Unfortunately, my chair was attached to my desk. This made moving even just an inch a big, loud production that the entire class heard, including Mr. Beller.

The first time it happened, I noticed his back stiffen, but he chose to ignore it. The second time Mr. Beller spun around and asked, "What's the problem here?"

And not in a nice way, either.

I froze. The class went silent. Mr. Beller's eyes narrowed in on mine, like he knew I was to blame. But rather than say anything, he turned back to the board.

Tobias was tall and his legs were long. I got kicked over and over again.

He only stopped when I turned around and watched him, so I did that for a while.

This wasn't the perfect solution, since it kept me from following what Mr. Beller was saying. But I figured I could always borrow Claire's notes later on. She sat at the other end of the room, in the kick-free zone.

Everyone but me seemed to occupy the kick-free zone.

"What are you staring at?" Tobias mumbled.

Before I could answer (not that I knew how to answer) Mr. Beller asked, "Is there a problem, Ms. Stevens?"

When teachers call you "Ms." anything, it's never a good sign.

I spun back around. "No, sir," I said, and for some reason, everyone laughed.

"Am I going to have to move you?"

I started to say no, but then I thought better of it. Anything to get me away from Tobias would be great.

"Actually, that would be nice, if it wouldn't be too much trouble."

He didn't say anything at first, so I closed my notebook, grabbed my backpack, and stood up. "Um, where should I go?"

Mr. Beller pointed to my chair, fuming now, but I didn't know why.

"Why don't you just sit yourself down where you were and move your desk back in line. We don't have time for your shenanigans."

"But I was just—"

I didn't even know what shenanigans Mr. Beller was talking about. The way he stared at me got me all choked up. I figured if I kept talking I'd cry, so I shut my mouth and slunk down in my chair.

Ten seconds later, Tobias pressed his foot into my back. He didn't kick me this time. He just maintained a constant pressure. I didn't turn around or try to stop him. Instead, I pretended that I was in a massage chair at Sharper Image. Like it was some great privilege to sit in front of Tobias, who provided me with this fabulous back rub, free of charge.

I took notes until the bell rang, setting us free not a second too soon. Then I rose from my chair carefully, like an old lady with creaky bones.

Claire waited for me outside. "What happened back there?" she asked.

I rubbed the small of my back with one hand, wondering if he'd left a bruise. "I don't know. How come Mr. Beller hates me?"

"Mostly because he's a jerk, but calling him 'sir' didn't help."

"I was being polite."

"Kids don't do that around here. He thought you were making fun of him. And then when you wanted to move seats . . ."

"He *asked* me if I wanted to."

"He was being sarcastic," Claire informed me.

"Oh." Now I felt dumb, but also angry. How was I supposed to know Mr. Beller wasn't serious? And how come everyone else—or at least Claire—realized it?

I stopped in front of my social studies room. "This is me."

Claire waved and said, "Don't worry about Mr. Beller, okay? I'll see you at lunch."

"See you."

I headed into class, almost bumping into a guy who walked out. He had long, scraggly, white-blond hair that was even paler than mine. Except for his bangs, which were dyed blue. He looked familiar but I couldn't place him. Well, not until he said, "Watch where you're going, Spazabelle," in a super nasty voice. Oh right, now I remembered. His name was Erik, and we had English, French, and math together. He and his friends shared our table at lunch, but it's not like we talked to them or anything.

"Sorry," I mumbled, ducking my head as I walked through the door.

Yesterday I was "Spamabelle." Today it's "Spaz-abelle." I wondered what he'd come up with next.

Sadly, I didn't have to wonder for long.

First thing Wednesday morning, Erik yelled, "Hey, Spaz," as I walked by his locker.

A couple of his friends overheard, and they cracked up, like it was the funniest thing they'd heard since sliced bread. Not that sliced bread is particularly funny, but you know what I mean. Anyway, they all thought he was *so* hilarious, they started calling me Spaz, too. Suddenly I couldn't walk down the hall or stand at my locker without having someone yell, "Spaz!"

The kicking, name calling, and general snubbing went on all week, but the biggest blow came on Friday afternoon during PE.

When our teacher, Ms. Chang, announced that we'd be starting a month-long basketball unit, I was beyond psyched. Okay, school was lousy. But playing basketball for forty-five minutes every day would definitely make things a little better. I volunteered to be team captain, but didn't get picked, which was no biggie. And I didn't get chosen first, but that was okay, too. No one at Birchwood knew that what I lacked in height, I made up for in speed and jumping ability. The reason I got so upset was because I got picked last. Dead last. After Maya Gilbert, who announced that no one was allowed to pass to her because she just got a French manicure. And after Jaden Ramsey, who had a broken arm. It was so humiliating! By the time the teams were sorted out, there wasn't time to play, so we just shot around. Or I should say, I *tried* to shoot around but no one would pass me the ball.

It was a fitting end to my rotten first week at Birchwood.

When I got home, I ran to the living room so I could set Stripe free from his kennel. And when I got there, I found him surrounded by a mess of fluffy white cotton. At first I wondered, "How'd my dog turn his kennel into a snow globe?" But when I got closer I realized he'd torn apart his pillow.

"Stripe, you were supposed to sleep on that, not eat it!"

I didn't know why I bothered explaining. He couldn't understand me. And from the way he marched back and forth, pacing the length of his kennel while letting out little yelping barks, it was clear he had other things on his mind. If he could talk he'd be yelling, "Get me out of this thing! I'm sick of being caged in."

"What's going on?" asked my mom, as she walked into the room. Once she took it all in she cried, "Oh, Stripe. How could you?"

"Sorry," I said.

"It's not your fault," Mom said. "And go ahead and take him outside. You can clean this up later."

I wasn't about to argue with that. I opened up the kennel door. Stripe stepped out and shook, sending little puffs of cotton flying. Then he stretched and headed to the door.

At least he made it outside before he peed. That

meant he'd had an accident-free day, and it was already 3:30.

Outside, I tried out some of the new names from the list of possibilities I'd thought up. Anything was better than Dweeble's idea, but none seemed exactly perfect. Not when I said them out loud, anyway.

"Let's go, Rover," I called. I thought Rover might work because he liked to explore.

Stripe headed to another part of the yard without looking my way.

"Here, Zippy," I tried (because he was fast).

Zippy seemed okay on paper, but didn't sound so great out loud.

I picked up the tennis ball, bounced it twice, and threw it across the yard. Stripe ran after it, picked it up, and then dropped down next to it so he could gnaw on it.

"Hey, Teddy?" I asked. "Do you like the name Teddy?"

"Is that for Teddy Roosevelt?" asked Mom, who'd snuck up behind me.

"I was thinking teddy bear, but I guess it could be for both," I said.

"Actually, the teddy bear was named after Teddy Roosevelt back when he was president."

"Really?" I asked. "That's cool, but I thought you taught English, not history."

"Very funny. And speaking of school, don't you want to get started on your homework?"

"Define want."

"Homework or unpacking," she said. "It's your choice."

"But it's Friday night," I argued.

"Exactly. You may as well finish up both so you can enjoy the rest of the weekend."

"Fine," I said. "It's okay to take Stripe upstairs, right?"

"As long as you watch him carefully, and don't let him eat anything weird. He got into the garbage again last night and swallowed an orange peel. Then this morning, he chewed a hole in one of Ted's favorite running socks."

"Wait. Ted has favorite *socks*?" I asked.

"Annabelle."

"Oh, come on," I said. "You have to admit that's nuts."

"I'll admit nothing," she said, all fancy and British.

I responded in my regular voice because I wasn't in the mood. "Okay, fine."

I finished up my homework that night, and unpacking took most of the next day.

Saturday night as I headed downstairs, I heard an awful sound blasting through the door to the den. I poked my head inside and found Dweeble sitting on the floor, attaching wires to one of his giant speakers. All his stuff was so big: his TV, his stereo equipment, his shoes.

"What are you listening to?" I asked, resisting the urge to cover my ears, but just barely.

"What?" Dweeble asked, pointing to his ear.

Since he couldn't hear me over the noise, I yelled, "Your music stinks!" at the top of my lungs.

Except I said it right after Dweeble turned down the volume.

My screaming surprised us both.

"Sorry." I blinked.

"No problem," Dweeble replied, trying not to laugh. I insult the guy and he thinks it's funny? Weird.

"What is that, anyway?"

"Meatloaf," he replied.

"I don't mean dinner. I mean the music." Even calling it music was a stretch, but I was trying to be on my best behavior.

"The guy singing is called Meatloaf," said Dweeble. He grabbed a remote and turned the volume back up.

"Does it have to be so loud?" I asked.

"Yes. Meatloaf always must be blasted. It's a great music rule." As a guitar solo blasted from the speakers, Dweeble played a little air guitar.

Wow, my mom sure knew how to pick 'em.

"I think I'm more into the vegetarians of rock bands. The Black Eyed Peas, the Red Hot Chili Peppers, that kind of thing."

"Hey, that's a good one," said Dweeble.

Dweeble thought I was funny? Not a good sign.

I headed into the kitchen, where Mom was making shrimp and vegetable kebabs.

"Oh, Annabelle. Can you please get me a red pepper from the fridge?"

"Pepper," I repeated. Suddenly it dawned on me.

"They're in the vegetable drawer. Make sure it's a red one, not orange."

"That's perfect," I said.

"Well, I'm glad you're so enthusiastic about our dinner," said Mom.

"No." I turned to face her. "Pepper is the perfect new name for Stripe."

Mom looked up and squinted, like she was trying to read an eye chart on the other side of the kitchen. "Pepper. Because of his coloring, you mean?"

Dweeble had described Stripe's not quite black and not quite white patches as "salt and pepper," but I'd only just now made the connection.

"Yup. And because I like the Red Hot Chili Peppers." Just then another cool reason popped into my head. "And because he's got pep."

Mom seemed excited. "Oh, and my favorite Beatles album is *Sgt. Pepper's Lonely Hearts Club Band*."

Feeling generous, I said, "Okay, fine. It can be for that, too."

I turned around and headed for the backyard.

"Where are you going?" my mom called.

"To tell Stripe about his new name."

"Well, can you get me the pepper first?"

"Oh, right! Sorry." I pulled out Mom's pepper and then ran upstairs to get the dog-training book. Turns out there was a whole chapter called "Naming Your Dog."

Use positive reinforcement to get your dog to learn his name. How so? Teach your dog that hearing his name means something amazing and fantastic is about to happen. What do dogs find fantastic? Um, can you say "being fed"? Fill your pockets with treats. Say your dog's name, then say *good boy*, and immediately give him a treat.

Rinse and repeat. Except skip the rinsing part. This is a dog-training book. Not a hair-shampooing instruction manual. Also, make sure you're not in the same place every time you call your dog by his name. He needs to learn that his name applies everywhere.

It was funny how much training involved food. I left the book in my room and ran downstairs to get Stripe. I mean Pepper.

I brought out some little bone-shaped biscuits and got to work.

"Pepper, come."

When he ran over I said, "Pepper, sit," and he totally listened.

"Good Pepper." I scratched him behind his ears and then walked to the other side of the yard.

"Here, Pepper," I called and he came.

Or at least, he started to come but then got sidetracked.

"Wait. Don't chew on the hose. No, Pepper. Stop."

When he dropped it I said, "Good Pepper."

He seemed to like his new name. Or at least, he liked getting fed. We practiced until I ran out of treats. And we kept practicing all weekend.

I kept my voice strong and firm the entire time. The commands came from deep within and there was a force behind my words.

By Sunday, Pepper knew his name, and he behaved like a model dog. Well, except for when he stole a chicken bone off Dweeble's plate, but there's an exception to every rule. Right?

That night, I ordered him to sit before opening the door. I made him sit before I put on his leash, and I made him sit before I fed him dinner.

The stricter I acted, the better he got.

chapter seven
dog-speak

Something weird happened at school on Monday. As soon as Tobias's foot made contact with my chair, I turned around and said, "Tobias, stop."

I didn't think about what I was doing first. The words just came out bossy before I could stop myself.

And Tobias actually looked at me. He seemed surprised and a little alarmed, like he didn't know me. Like he heard something different in my voice, and maybe realized I was someone he didn't want to mess with.

His stunned silence didn't last long, though. Within seconds his features twisted back into a look of annoyance.

"What?" he asked.

"Cut it out," I snapped.

Tobias waited, but just for a few minutes. Clearly he wasn't about to give up that easily.

The next time he kicked me I turned around and spoke even more forcefully. "I said, stop kicking my chair!" I didn't mean to be so loud, but from the way the entire class stared, it was clear that everyone heard me.

"What's with the ruckus?" asked Mr. Beller.

I quickly faced forward. My first instinct was to stay silent and pretend like nothing was the matter. That was the easiest thing to do. But it wasn't fair that I should get in trouble, when all I did was sit there and try to pay attention.

It wasn't me causing the ruckus. And who used a word like *ruckus,* anyway? It was even dumber than calling something a *shenanigan.*

Something bubbled up from deep inside me. I don't know where it came from, or what it was, exactly. Last week I would've apologized softly. Last week, I'd have done anything to deflect the class's attention. But something had changed.

I took a deep breath and said, "I'm sorry, sir. I mean, Mr. Beller. I didn't mean to cause a ruckus. I was just asking Tobias to please stop kicking my chair, because it's distracting."

Behind me, Tobias groaned.

"Mr. Miller," said our teacher. "Are you kicking Annabelle's chair?"

Tobias stayed silent. All eyes were on us. I didn't want to be a snitch, but he'd left me with no choice. Another few weeks of the kicking and I might develop a case of serious whiplash. Okay, perhaps that's a stretch, but still. The guy was annoying, and I couldn't let him get away with it anymore.

I heard the sounds of muffled giggles but for once I didn't care.

"Tobias?" our teacher asked.

"Don't worry about it, Mr. Beller," I said. "I was probably mistaken. Maybe it was just the wind, or something."

A few students laughed, Claire included.

An annoyed Mr. Beller looked from Tobias to me. "Well, then. Everyone pull out your homework and pass it to the front. I trust there won't be any more interruptions."

As Mr. Beller blabbed on about the correct format for our book reports, due in just a couple of weeks, I watched the second hand sweep its way around the face of the clock. One minute went by, then two. Tobias didn't kick.

I sat up straight and took notes. Amazingly, I made it to the end of class without feeling like someone's kickboxing target. When the bell rang, I gathered my things.

Tobias left fast with his books tucked under one arm. "See you in science," I called after him, just because I could. Tobias ignored me, but I didn't care.

I sailed through social studies and the rest of the morning. At lunch, Claire told everyone how I'd gotten Tobias into trouble. "He was shocked. It was like no one had ever challenged him before. She was awesome."

"How did you do it?" asked Emma, staring at me carefully.

"I don't know," I said with a shrug. "It just sort of happened."

"Impressive," said Rachel.

"Totally," Yumi agreed.

"It wasn't a big deal," I told them. But the thing is, it was.

As soon as the bell rang, I hurried to science, excited because we'd finally get to use the lab equipment this week.

When I sat down, Ms. Roberts passed out microscopes—one for each lab group. We also got a small envelope that contained six numbered slides. We were supposed to take turns looking at each slide so we could write down our observations. For homework, we needed to try and figure out what we were looking at.

Not to sound like a nerd or anything, but I was excited, because the assignment was like a puzzle and I'm into that sort of thing.

When our microscope landed on our table, I had to smile. This wasn't like the cheap plastic one I got for my eighth birthday that melted into an orange puddle two weeks later. (Never bring a plastic microscope to the beach, and definitely don't leave it in your mom's car on one of the hottest days of summer.) This microscope was heavy and serious looking, a real piece of scientific equipment. I thought so, anyway.

But before I could get my hands on the thing,

Tobias grabbed it and slid it to his side of the table. "I'll go first," he said.

My smile quickly faded. I was about to protest, when someone whispered, "Spaz," from the table behind us.

As the guys snickered, I hunched into myself and pretended like I didn't hear.

Tobias slipped the first slide in, bent over the viewfinder, and peered inside. I watched him adjust the side dials, bringing the tray closer to the lens. I was curious, but didn't want to get too close. Anyway, I figured I'd have a turn soon enough.

A few seconds later, Oliver stood up and walked to the other side of Tobias. He leaned in, with his elbows resting on the edge of the table. "Let's see," he said.

"Hold on." Tobias kept one hand on the arm of the microscope and used the other to shield it from Oliver.

At least he acted rude to us both.

"Come on," said Oliver. He seemed so anxious, I almost felt bad for the guy.

Tobias finally passed him the microscope. Oliver peered through and said, "Whoa."

"What?" I asked.

They ignored me.

Tobias took down his notes.

Oliver kept looking. "That's pretty cool," he said.

"I know," Tobias replied.

"Let me see."

Oliver tried to pass me the microscope but Tobias pulled it away and grabbed the next slide.

"Wait, I didn't get a turn," I said, which shouldn't have been necessary. I mean it was obvious I hadn't seen it.

"Too late, Spazabelle." Tobias pointed to the clock. "We're running out of time."

He stared me down, challenging me to object, but I couldn't.

I watched them go from slide to slide to slide, and I didn't say a word.

Tobias wrote down his observations with my pen. He didn't even ask this time. He just saw it sitting there and took it. When I tried to see what he was writing, he blocked his page with his elbow.

They let me look at the last two slides, but only because Ms. Roberts strolled by our table and asked how we were all doing. Slide number five looked like little gray scratches on glass. Slide number six looked like bigger scratches. I'm sure it all would've made more sense if I'd seen the sequence from the beginning, but now I had no idea what I was look-ing at. I told myself it didn't matter. I could always ask Yumi later on, since she had Ms. Roberts first period. But that wasn't the point. I was mad at the boys for hogging the microscope for the entire class. And I was mad at myself, too, because I let them.

I wish I knew what came over me in English

class. Why had it been so easy to stand up to Tobias then?

I couldn't figure it out.

Not until I got home and took Pepper for a walk.

Before I opened the front door I said, "Pepper, sit." And I hardly recognized my own voice.

It's because my tone sounded different—stronger and more commanding. I was only following the instructions. My dog-training book said I had to talk to Pepper like that so he'd actually listen. And it worked.

But here's the thing: I'd talked to Tobias that way, too.

The dog-training lesson worked on a boy.

Wow. Just thinking about the possibilities made my brain spin. When I first met Pepper, he was wild and unruly. Just like Tobias and the other middle school boys.

With my dog, all I had to do was learn some rules, pitch my voice a certain way, and give him commands. Pepper's behavior got better every day.

It got me thinking. . . . Was it actually possible to train boys like I trained my dog?

Yes, it already had worked on Tobias this morning. But could it work on other boys, too?

And what about the other lessons? Would they apply?

I ran upstairs, sat down at my desk, and opened up the book. Taking a pencil, I crossed out the word "dog" and replaced it with "boy."

UNDERSTANDING ~~DOG~~ Boy-SPEAK

Talk to ~~dogs~~ boys in their own language. Your tone is just as important as your words. *Stay? Sit? Come?* Don't ask them. Tell them. You're the boss, so act that way. Make your commands firm, short, and to the point. This is how you'll get ~~dogs~~ boys to listen to you.

It totally made sense! I flipped through the book, looking for other lessons to adapt, and found plenty: positive reinforcement, bribery, walking on a leash. Okay, maybe not walking on a leash, but the others would work. This was amazing. Monumental. Completely awesome. If I could actually pull it off, that is.

Just reading about it made me feel better.

Later that night, Mom poked her head into my room. "You're studying hard," she said.

I grinned. "Well, like you said, sixth grade is a lot of work."

She smiled back. "I was going to remind you to take Pepper outside before you went to bed, but since you're working, I'll do it myself."

"Okay, thanks," I said.

When she brought the dog back into my room, I was almost halfway done translating the book.

"It's getting late, Annabelle."

I yawned. "I'll go to bed soon."

"Okay, good. Sleep tight." She kissed my forehead and then headed out.

I finished one more chapter, changed into my pajamas, and got into bed. I was plenty tired but too excited to sleep. For the first time since I started going to Birchwood, I couldn't wait until school.

chapter eight
boy-speak

I got so caught up in studying I forgot to put Pepper in his kennel for the night. He woke me up at six thirty the next morning by jumping on my bed and licking my ear.

"Oh, gross. Pepper, cut it out." I rolled over and buried my head under my pillow. But he wouldn't let up and pushed his wet nose into my neck.

"It's too early," I groaned.

Next he swatted my shoulder with one paw. I turned to face him and noticed something green caught on the fur near his collar. "What's that?" I leaned closer to get a better look. Pepper was sporting a piece of lettuce on his neck. And he smelled like garbage.

I threw off the covers, jumped out of bed, and ran downstairs. Turns out Pepper had tipped over the kitchen trash and had helped himself to everything inside. Remnants of last night's dinner littered the entire room, along with banana peels, eggshells, chewed up paper towels, and stuff I didn't even recognize.

"Oh, Pepper, this is disgusting."

He wagged his tail, hard. He seemed completely unconcerned. Just like he did two days ago, when he stole one of mom's used tissues out of the bathroom trash. I'll never get used to the fact that the little guy actually enjoyed eating garbage—maybe even more than he liked his kibble. There wasn't any point in scolding him, though. According to the dog-training book, dogs have short memories.

> If you don't catch your dog in the act of doing something wrong, there's no use in yelling at him, because he'll have no idea what he's being punished for.

So I cleaned up the mess before Mom and Dweeble found it. Then I led Pepper outside and got ready for school.

After reviewing my notes in the car, I felt ready for English. Before Tobias could even think about bugging me, I stared him down.

"What?" he asked.

I looked him straight in the eye, because I figured it would be intimidating. I made sure to speak clearly and used few words, since his vocabulary might not be so great. "Don't kick."

He looked at me like he thought I was nuts. "Geez, Spaz. What makes you think I was going to kick you?"

Um, maybe because you spent all last week

kicking me? I didn't ask him out loud, though. This wasn't a conversation. It was an order.

"I'm just saying, don't," I replied. "And don't call me Spaz. My name is Annabelle."

The dog-training book had instructions on how to teach Pepper his own name, but it didn't cover teaching Pepper *my* name. And I couldn't figure out how to reverse the lesson with Tobias, so I figured I'd just tell him.

"Whatever," Tobias mumbled.

Pepper never talked back, but I guess I couldn't expect a perfect translation.

Mr. Beller called the class to attention, so I turned around. He collected our homework and I didn't get kicked. He started talking about how we could expand our vocabulary by reading more and I still didn't get kicked. Then he named three students who'd forgotten to turn in their homework on Monday. I wasn't on his list but Tobias was. Oh, and I still didn't get kicked.

I tried not to make a big deal out of it. I didn't want to get too comfortable. That had been my mistake yesterday. After one small victory, I'd let my guard down. Boys, like dogs, needed reinforcement. It wasn't enough to teach Pepper to sit once. I had to remind him to do it over and over again. This meant my work was far from finished.

Since I still had five more classes to get through, plus lunch, I tried to think in positive terms. Like, instead of having hours of potential torture ahead of me, I had that much more opportunity for boy training.

It worked for a while. Then, as I walked to my locker to get my social studies book, some guy yelled, "Spaz!"

It would have been easy to walk by and pretend that I didn't hear, or didn't know he was talking to me. That's what I did yesterday. And that's what I'd done all last week. But ignoring the problem wasn't going to change anything.

So rather than slink off silently, I turned around and followed him. Once I got close enough, I tapped him on the shoulder and said, "Hey, wait."

"Huh?" The guy spun around, pushing his dark hair away from his forehead with one hand. He seemed confused and not exactly thrilled that I'd stopped him. He was taller than me, but practically everyone at Birchwood was. I couldn't let that stop me.

"Did you say something?" I asked.

He looked at me like I was crazy. Like I was speaking to him in Spanish when he was barely passing French. "No," he said, and tried to walk away.

"Wait a sec." I grabbed onto the sleeve of his jacket, then pulled my hand away, surprised that I could be so gutsy.

"What?" he asked, now annoyed, staring where my hand had been as if I'd left a stain.

I lost my train of thought. I tried to visualize Pepper tearing up the garden, not because he didn't like my mom, but just because he didn't know any better.

Dogs need to be told what to do. They don't know, instinctively.

Maybe boys were the same.

"You called me Spaz, just now, and that's not my name."

His cheeks flushed red and his eyes darted from left to right. He refused to meet my gaze. "I don't even know you," he insisted.

"My point exactly," I said. "And let's keep it that way."

By the time I got to our regular table at lunch, everyone else was already there. I had to squeeze into the only space available, which happened to be between Rachel and Erik. This week, his bangs were green. I didn't know if it was an entirely new color, or if the blue had faded, but it's not like I could ask him. The guy was way hostile.

Example? As soon as I sat down he asked, "Do you mind, Spaz?"

I guess he was upset that I was crowding him, but the thing is—there were five of us girls, and only four boys, and they took up way more than half the table. He could've easily moved over. There was plenty of room—but I didn't say so. I didn't want to try any boy training in front of an audience. It was all too new. And what would Rachel and her friends think? Obviously they were okay with being smushed. Or maybe they'd gone to school with boys for so long, they didn't realize how annoying they were.

Anyway, I ignored Erik, and he soon got distracted by his friend Joe, a short skinny kid with curly dark hair, braces, and pimples all over his forehead.

"Five bucks says you can't fit that entire corn dog into your mouth," said Joe.

Erik laughed, brushed his green bangs out of his eyes and said, "Dude, that's easy." Then he lifted the corn dog and slowly shoved it into his mouth. His cheeks bulged, contorting his entire face. Somehow, and I don't know how, he stuffed it all in.

The other boys watched in awe.

"Do you know what hot dogs are made out of?" Claire whispered. "Random pig parts, like intestines, and brains, and pieces of bone."

Yumi put down her corn dog in disgust. "That's not true," she said. "Is it?"

"It could be lips, too. Basically, hot dogs are made out of spare parts that no one else wanted," she went on.

I was glad I'd gotten the fried chicken. Sure, it was soggy, but at least I could tell I was eating a leg as opposed to lips. If chickens even had lips. Did beaks function in the same way? And if so, could they be called chicken lips? I'd have to Google that later.

"Claire is a vegetarian," said Rachel. "Whatever you do, don't ask her about veal."

"Or factory farm chickens," Emma added.

"You should see their crowded cages. They cram so many inside, the chickens don't even have room to turn around," said Claire.

I put down my chicken and reached for my chips. "Just don't tell me anyone abused these potatoes," I said, and everyone laughed.

Suddenly Erik started coughing. A large chunk of corn dog flew out of his mouth and landed on the table—inches from my lunch. If Claire was right, I hoped it wasn't the pig lips part.

I leaned away from it, just in case.

Meanwhile, Joe stood up and raised his hands over his head. "Yes, I won!" he yelled.

"No, I got it all in," Erik insisted.

"What do you call that?" asked Joe, pointing to the corn dog remains.

Erik shook his head. "That wasn't the bet. I got it all in at once."

"But you didn't eat it all."

"Fine," Erik said.

Much to my horror (and okay, I'll admit it— fascination, too) he picked the piece up off the table and popped it into his mouth.

As Joe pulled some crumpled bills out of his pocket and slammed them on the table, the other boys cheered.

Next someone dared Erik to drink chocolate milk mixed with ketchup, salt, pepper, relish, and mayonnaise. This he did free of charge.

After he downed it, he burped and pounded his chest. "I'm a human garbage disposal!" he roared. Like eating trash was something to brag about.

Just then I remembered Pepper, wagging his tail

happily in the midst of the kitchen garbage. These boys really were just like dogs.

I giggled at the thought.

"What's so funny?" asked Rachel.

"Um, nothing," I said, since it was too complicated to explain. I finished my lunch quickly and left our table early so I could hide in the bathroom and go over my notes before class.

Science would be tough, because I was outnumbered, with boys on either side of me and behind me, too. So I needed the extra time to get ready.

🐾 LEADING THE PACK 🐾

Dogs [Boys] are pack animals. They relate to one another in groups. Confused? Think about it this way: your teacher is your class leader. He or she tells you what to do and you listen. Right?

Dogs [Boys] have leaders, too. And as far as dogs [boys] see the world, there are leaders and there are followers. There is nothing in between. Even in a pack of two, there's a hierarchy: a dominant dog [boy] who's boss, and a submissive dog [boy] who follows.

You must become the dominant person of your pack.

In science, Ms. Roberts was the obvious pack leader, since she decided what we'd do, and assigned homework and stuff. Basically, she gave orders that we carried out.

But the class had other packs, as well. Like at

Table Number Seven—clearly, Tobias was the leader. He took control, and Oliver just watched and waited to be told what to do. Oliver wasn't a bad guy, I don't think. It was more like he was just trying to fit in. I had a feeling that if Tobias were nice to me, he would be, too, which was a little sad, but still irritating.

Clearly Tobias was the dominant dog and Oliver was the submissive dog. And me? I was neither dog. Not even a follower because they didn't bother acknowledging me. If anything, I guess I could be called the invisible dog. And that had to change.

By the time I walked into class, the microscopes were on the table. Tobias was already fitting the first slide into place, while Oliver watched.

I took a deep breath and marched forward.

"I'll take that," I said, holding out my hand.

"What?" asked Tobias.

"I'll do that," I said. "Since I didn't get a real turn yesterday." He didn't volunteer to give up control, so I grabbed the microscope and pulled it in front of me.

Tobias took it back just as fast. "Cut it out, Spazzers."

Okay, that hadn't gone so well.

"Come on," I said.

Don't ask your dog to do something. Tell him. . . .

The words ran through my head as I reached for the microscope, again.

"I'm going first." I spoke decisively. And this time, I managed to grab hold of the neck.

Tobias kept both hands on its base. He just wouldn't let go, and neither would I.

Soon we were playing tug-of-war, both of us pulling as hard as we could. At least until Ms. Roberts came over.

Tobias saw her first and let go immediately.

Me? I held on and went flying past our table and into the aisle. Before I could stop myself I slammed hard into the sidewall.

I didn't fall or drop the microscope, but no one focused on that. Everyone was too busy laughing over the spectacle I'd made of myself.

"What's going on here?" Ms. Roberts asked. "Am I going to have to separate you two?"

Yes, please separate us, I thought to myself, as I walked back to my seat and gently placed the microscope on the table.

I didn't agree out loud, because I'd already gotten into trouble for that in English class. I don't understand these teachers, asking questions and then getting mad when you try and agree with them, but I wasn't going to say so.

Ms. Roberts stared from me to Tobias, like she was trying to figure out who to blame.

Neither of us said a word.

When she finally spoke her tone was harsh. "Please get back to work. And try to remember that you're in the sixth grade now, and it's time to act that way."

For the rest of the class, I let Tobias be the dominant dog.

He lingered over each slide first and only let me and Oliver peek after he'd finished. It didn't feel great, but this was only my first official day of boy training. I figured I deserved a little slack.

Five minutes before class ended, Ms. Roberts asked, "How many people did the reading last night?"

When I raised my hand, Tobias poked me in the side.

"Ow," I said, even though it didn't really hurt all that much. Just, the surprise of it got to me. "Stop," I whispered.

But he faced forward, ignoring me. Pepper wouldn't pull a move like that, so I didn't know how to deal with it.

"For three extra-credit points, who can tell me what it's called when plants absorb energy from sunlight?" she asked.

Photosynthesis. The answer popped into my brain, and I knew, I just knew I was right but I didn't say so. Volunteering to speak seemed too risky. I figured I'd be better off laying low until I perfected the boy training. Instead, I stared down at my open notebook and started doodling, without really paying attention to what I was doing.

"No one knows the answer?" asked Ms. Roberts.

A few hands trickled up.

Suddenly the air to my left shifted. Tobias waved his arm back and forth, desperate to be called on. "Oh, oh, oh, I know!" He wiggled in his chair like he couldn't keep the answer to himself and would absolutely explode into a hundred pieces if he didn't get it out right that second.

Ms. Roberts called on him.

"It's photosynthesis," he said, grinning like mad, and entirely too pleased with himself.

He was right. I knew he was right. But he didn't have to make such a big deal about it. It's not like he was the only one who knew.

Still, our teacher looked impressed. "Well done, Tobias."

I wondered. Had Tobias been playing dumb all this time, or had he finally decided to do his homework?

After Ms. Roberts moved on, Tobias looked at me and whispered, "Thanks, Spaz."

"Huh?" I asked.

"Thanks for the answer." He pointed to my open notebook, where I'd written *photosynthesis* without even realizing it.

Staring at the word, the horrible truth dawned on me. Rather than becoming the dominant dog, I'd helped the dominant dog get extra credit, while landing myself in the doghouse with our teacher.

Clearly I had a lot to learn.

chapter nine
dominant dogs

"So do you have a boyfriend yet?"

"Sophia, you have to stop asking me that every single day."

"I know. That's why I skipped yesterday."

"That's only because I didn't call you back," I said. "And anyway, my answer isn't going to change, I promise."

"Someday it will," said Sophia.

"Did you only call me to talk about boys?"

"No, I called to tell you we can't come over this weekend."

"Oh, no. How come?"

"We don't have a ride. Mia's dad is out of town and her mom's car is in the shop and my parents are too busy."

I groaned. I only lived thirty miles away. It's not like me and Mom moved to Mars. "What about your sister?"

"She's grounded because she missed her curfew again. My parents won't even let her use the car to take me places."

"That stinks."

"I know. I'm really sorry. They promised to take us next Friday, right from school. If that's okay with you."

"Of course."

"Maybe by then you'll have a boyfriend."

I groaned. "Not funny."

"It kind of was. I'll call you tomorrow, okay?"

"Sure, bye."

As much as I missed Sophia, I was happy to get off the phone. All she ever wanted to talk about were the Birchwood boys. Meanwhile, I had the opposite problem with Mia. We'd only talked once since I'd moved. And for some reason, we didn't even have that much to say to each other. I know Mia doesn't like talking on the phone—or talking much in general, for that matter. But I was hoping she'd make an exception.

As bummed out as I was about not seeing my friends this weekend, I tried to look on the bright side. At least that left me more time for studying. I cracked open my dog-training manual and flipped to the next lesson.

True, things hadn't gone entirely as planned, but I'd done okay with Tobias when we were alone. And just yesterday, I confronted three more random guys who called me "Spaz." (Okay, that meant I'd stopped five out of at least twelve, but it was a start.)

I'd only read half of the book and hoped that more answers lay hidden inside. And sure enough, one mistake soon became clear. I'd tried to become

the dominant dog in science without actually knowing what that meant.

Meanwhile, the definition was spelled out for me.

❧ How to Be the Dominant Dog ❧

Think about it this way: in a group of dogs, you can
always spot a dominant dog in a pack by his swagger. He walks with his chest pushed forward, confi-
dently. His ears are pointy and alert, and he looks
straight ahead. This designated leader is in control,
and he decides what everyone else should do.
While the dominant dog stays ahead, the more
submissive dogs—the followers of the pack—will
walk behind.

When you're with your dog, be the designated
leader. Make sure your dog is walking behind you
or next to you, but never in front of you. This way,
he'll know that you're in control.

Dominant dogs have a swagger. Dominant boys
know how to strut.

As I read the words, I could just picture Jackson
walking down the hall with confidence and control,
like he owned the whole school, like he could do
whatever he wanted to do.

Lots of boys at Birchwood acted this way—come
to think of it, plenty of girls, did too. And because
they had this attitude, people let them get away
with anything. Which just gave them more of an attitude, and more power.

Then I thought about how I'd been walking around school—rushing from place to place, totally lost and confused, my eyes on the ground, my posture hesitant and even slouchy. I hugged my books tightly against my chest. In trying to become invisible, so no one would tease me, I'd acted totally weak. No wonder boys picked on me. I was sending out wimpy signals.

But maybe it wasn't too late to change. Maybe I could learn how to swagger. I stood up and walked across the room with my head back and my shoulders swaying. Okay, it felt weird, and I probably looked dorky, but at least I had time to practice.

That night at dinner, Pepper sat at my feet, whining and begging and watching every bite of food as it traveled from my plate to my mouth. Just to see what would happen, I waved my empty fork around in the air. He followed that, too.

"Maybe we should put him back in the kennel," said Dweeble.

"He'll be there all night," I argued. "It's not fair."

"We really need to teach him not to beg," said Mom.

"I'll add it to the list," I replied tiredly, as I pushed a cherry tomato across my plate.

"So tell me more about school," Mom said.

"There's nothing to tell."

"Oh, come on. It's middle school. You have six new teachers and lots of new friends."

"I do not."

"What about Rachel and all those other girls you've been eating lunch with?"

My mom was trying too hard, which was never a good thing.

"They're her friends."

"You know, Jason went to Birchwood," Dweeble said, out of nowhere.

"What?" I asked.

"My son, Jason, from my first marriage."

Mom told me that Dweeble had a son, but I didn't know much about him. Only that his bedroom was down the hall from mine, and when he stayed over (which my mom said would hardly ever happen) we'd share a bathroom. But wait a second.

"How many marriages have you had?" I asked.

Dweeble laughed and winked at my mom. "Just the one, so far."

I turned to my mom. "I thought you told me Jason was from Oregon."

"He goes to Reed College up in Portland, Oregon, but he grew up here in Westlake," Dweeble explained. "And actually, he's studying abroad in Switzerland this year."

"Ted's going to visit him soon," said Mom.

"Really? For how long?" I tried not to sound too excited, but I couldn't help it. Switzerland is all the way in Europe, which is really far from here.

"Just a week," Dweeble told me. "Saturday to Saturday, which should be enough time to get in some decent skiing."

"I haven't skied in years," said my mom. "And Annabelle hasn't ever been."

"Well, we'll have to change that," said Dweeble. "What do you say we head up to Tahoe this winter?"

I didn't know what to say. Winter was months away. And moving in with Dweeble was a big deal. Now we're planning vacations with him, too? It was so much to think about.

"You okay, Annabelle?" My mom reached over and squeezed my arm.

I shrugged. "I'm fine, I guess."

Dweeble smiled at me. "Being the new kid is tough, but you'll get used to it."

I'd heard that before but it didn't make me feel any better. I didn't particularly want to get used to being picked on.

"Can I please be excused?" I asked.

"Don't you want dessert?" asked Dweeble. He got up and headed to the pantry, coming back a minute later with a fancy-looking silver box. "I picked up some Swiss chocolate at the new gourmet food store."

He flipped back the lid to reveal rows of chocolate pieces—some milk, some dark, and all delicious looking. "These were imported from Lucerne, the small town where Jason is living. I figured eating them would remind me of him."

Even though I made fun of Dweeble all the time, I had to admit there was something sweet about this. More importantly, the chocolates were delicious— hard on the outside and melty on the inside. When I caught one between the roof of my mouth and my tongue and pressed up, the flavor spread everywhere, making my taste buds go crazy.

"So good," I said.

My mom took a piece too, even though she was still working on her steak. "Delicious."

Dweeble agreed. "Yes, cheese, chocolate, fondue, and universal health care. They really know what they're doing in Switzerland."

Whatever that meant.

Pepper sniffed at the table.

"Not for you," I said.

"Definitely not. Be careful with that," said Dweeble. "Chocolate is toxic for dogs. There's a chemical in it called theobromine that humans can digest, but dogs can't. In fact, too much could kill him."

"Really?" I asked, gulping.

"No joke." Dweeble moved the box to the center of the table, far from Pepper's reach. "It's a bad idea to feed dogs any human food, but if Pepper gets his hands on chocolate, onions, or grapes, we've got a serious problem."

"Good thing he doesn't have hands," I said.

Dweeble chuckled. "Right."

As I reached for a second piece, I realized something. Chocolate may be dangerous for dogs . . . but it's probably okay for boys.

chapter ten
boy treats

The next day, I strutted into science class, walking tall, with my shoulders swaying. I tried to adopt Jackson's bouncy heeled swagger, and hoped I didn't look too ridiculous. I didn't know how to translate the pointy ears into something I could use to my advantage, but I didn't want to skip any steps. So just to be safe, I visualized that my ears were pointy.

Unfortunately, I got to class too early, wasting my alpha-dog swagger. No one got to see it except for the teacher, and she hardly looked up from the paper she was grading.

"Hi, Ms. Roberts."

"Hello, Annabelle," she replied.

Since I wasn't one for small talk I made my way to Table Number Seven and sat down. Luckily, the new walk wasn't my only strategy. All this time, I'd forgotten one of the most basic principles of dog training. Dogs respond to food. Hopefully boys would, too.

I reached into my backpack and pulled out two

pieces of Dweeble's fancy Swiss chocolate. Just holding them made my mouth water, like Pepper's did whenever he saw me go for the dog biscuits.

As hard as the chocolate was to part with, I knew it had to be done. This was too important. If it worked, it would be worth the sacrifice.

I placed one piece in front of Oliver's space and one piece in front of Tobias's.

Call it bribery or call it positive reinforcement. I didn't care, as long as it worked.

As the class filled up, I went over my notes. (I had time to glance at both sets—the science ones and the boy ones.)

"What's this?" asked Tobias, as soon as he sat down. He picked up the candy and held it closer to his face. Like maybe he thought the answer to his question was written on the wrapper in tiny print. (It wasn't. The answer was in my brain. Oh, and in the dog/boy-training book, of course.)

I smiled through gritted teeth, pretending like I didn't find him to be the most annoying guy in the world. "It's this really great chocolate from Switzerland. My mom's boyfriend got it for me."

"And you're giving me this?"

"Sure." I nodded and looked him in the eye.

He stared back, trying to figure out why I was being nice to him, I guess. Well, I'd wonder, too.

I shrugged and faked a smile. "We have so much of it at home, I just want to unload some. Plus, I thought you and Oliver would like it." I kept talking since he wasn't. "Go ahead and try it. It's really good."

Tobias eyed the candy, like he was afraid I'd poisoned it or something. The boy treats didn't seem to be working, which was a problem, because I didn't have a backup plan.

I was about to give up—to tell him I was kidding, or to just not say anything—when the final bell rang.

Suddenly Oliver bounded into the room, red faced, out of breath, and a little sweaty, too. He slammed his books on our table, saw the candy, and said, "Oh, sweet!" Then he unwrapped it and popped it into his mouth.

We both watched Oliver chomp and swallow. He didn't savor the candy like I thought he would. In fact, he probably ate it too fast to recognize the greatness. I glanced from one boy to the other, worried that I'd wasted fancy chocolate for nothing.

Tobias studied Oliver with suspicion. After a minute passed and Oliver hadn't fallen to the floor, or foamed at the mouth, or sprouted a head-to-toe rash, I guess Tobias became convinced that I hadn't given him poison, so he ate his, too.

"Mmm." Tobias grunted. He spent more time chewing his piece, and seemed to appreciate it on some deeper level, which almost made me like him. Almost.

"You're welcome," I said.

Neither of them said thanks, but I know they heard me. And guess what? I didn't care. And guess what else? When we had to do a group experiment, we actually did a group experiment.

It's because I stayed in dominant dog mode, grabbing the microscope and saying to Tobias, "I'll look first, and tell you what I see."

When Oliver started to protest I told him, "You can take notes for the table."

I don't know if it was the chocolate bribe or my tone of voice, or maybe my ears were pointing in some small, subtle way. Whatever it was, it worked.

Tobias seemed too surprised to argue. I looked him straight in the eye, as if daring him to challenge me. And he didn't say a word.

Oliver actually opened up his notebook and took notes like I told him to.

Sure, he had to borrow my pen before he did it, but it was a start.

Anyway, after class, I made sure to get it back.

Now that the boy situations in English and science were under control, I figured everything else would be easy.

But a week later, when I got to our normal spot for lunch, Erik and his friends were already sitting there. (We called them the Corn Dog Boys now, for the obvious reasons.) For a second, I worried that someone had invited them to eat with us. Then I noticed Rachel and Claire standing off to the side. Rachel glared daggers at them. Claire always seemed so happy and easygoing, but today she looked like she was sucking on a sour ball.

"What's up?" I asked.

"We're just waiting for Yumi and Emma," said Claire, blowing her bangs out of her face with an annoyed huff. "And then we have to find somewhere else to sit."

"It's not fair. The Corn Dog Boys only beat me by, like, ten seconds." Rachel spoke in a whisper, and gestured toward the boys with her chin.

It's not like we hadn't seen it coming. Every day, the Corn Dog Boys edged further and further into our territory. Yesterday we'd bumped elbows with them. And today they'd taken over: spreading their backpacks around and splaying their legs wide, taking up way more space than they needed to take up.

"If they just moved a little, we could all fit," I said.

Claire giggled, nervously. "You can tell them that if you want, but I'm staying here."

"They can't just hog the whole area." Even as I said this, I knew full well the Corn Dog Boys could do whatever they wanted to do, because, well, I guess because no one would tell them otherwise. "We've been sitting there since the first day of school."

I thought Rachel would agree with me but she just shrugged silently.

I couldn't believe it. Rachel actually lived with a real live boy. She had plenty of opportunity to practice dealing with that species. The way she yelled at Jackson amazed me. Yet here she was, intimidated by a few sixth graders. I guess it was different when the boys in question weren't related to you.

Just then Emma came over asking, "What's up?" As soon as she noticed the Corn Dog Boys she froze, like an invisible force field protected them.

It was no shocker that Emma hung back. She seemed to survive junior high by keeping a low profile and staying out of every boy's way. Emma was a total braniac—a straight-A student in all honors classes. So maybe she was onto something. Of course, I'd tried to make myself invisible, too, but it didn't work for me.

We looked around at the mostly full lunch area. All the good spots were already taken. The only space large enough to fit the five of us was right next to the garbage cans. Flies buzzed nearby. Smelly trash overflowed onto the bench seats. No mystery why that spot remained empty.

Someone had to do something. We couldn't eat by garbage and we couldn't eat standing up. Yet we all just stood there.

"I'll be right back," I said and ducked behind a tree. I pulled out my dog/boy-training book and flipped through the pages in search of something that might help.

🐾 STRANGERS 🐾

When you approach a dog you don't know, do so carefully. Don't look him in the eye. He may take that to be a threat. Before you get too close, let him get to know you first. Stick out your hand, so he can sniff you. Let him make the first move. Then, once he seems comfortable, proceed to pet.

Hmm. That didn't exactly apply. Erik was no stranger. Just someone who I wished was a stranger. Especially since he was clearly the dominant dog in the Corn Dog Boy pack. And of course, I'd no interest in petting him.

I flipped to the next page.

🐾 Turf 🐾

Dogs are territorial. They are not natural hosts, who will smile kindly and invite you in for tea and crumpets. So never walk your dog into a strange dog's house. Two animals should meet on neutral ground, in a safe space first—one that neither dog can claim as their own. Let them get comfortable with each other, sniff each other out. This could take time. Whatever you do, don't rush things.

Well, that might work . . .

As a backup plan, I pulled a few pieces of Swiss chocolate out of my lunch bag. I didn't want to give up any more, but I couldn't deny that it'd worked like magic last week.

I approached the Corn Dog Boys carefully, not actually putting out my hand for them to sniff, of course, but sort of pretending to, just like I had with my pointy ears. When I got close enough I called out, "Hey."

Busy pelting each other with Cool Ranch Doritos, the boys didn't hear me. Or maybe they ignored me on purpose. Either way, I couldn't give up that easily. "Hey, Erik," I said, louder this time.

Erik finally looked up, but didn't say a word. Someone had cut his bangs, so now only the tips had a tint of faded green.

I started moving closer but stopped because I didn't want to startle him.

"Um, can I talk to you for a minute?"

"What?" he asked, sharply.

Don't ask, tell. I needed to be better about following the rules. I waved him closer. "Come here."

Erik rolled his eyes and started to stand up. But then Joe whispered something in his ear. The two of them laughed. I felt my cheeks heat up. I told myself I was lucky I didn't know what he said, that it didn't matter. Words were just words. I needed action.

"Come on, Erik." I used my most commanding tone of voice, pretending that I'd just caught Pepper chewing up my favorite T-shirt.

Amazingly, Erik stood up and headed over.

"What do you want?" He seemed annoyed, like his time was so precious and I'd interrupted his very important baloney sandwich consumption.

I leaned against the tree, like that could protect me, and glanced over my shoulder. My friends watched from a safe distance. By now Yumi had joined them. This didn't seem to be working, which made me want to give up, but it was too late. Turning back to face him, I took a deep breath and tried to make my case. "Um, we've been sitting there since the beginning of school, and since you're only four people taking up the whole table, I was wondering . . . Well, we were kind of hoping you and your friends could maybe move over. Just a little."

"We were here first."

There was too much hesitation in my voice, so I tried again. "There's room for everyone."

"Whatever." He turned to go.

"No, wait." I grabbed the sleeve of his T-shirt. He stopped and narrowed his eyes at me. Gasping, I dropped my hand, since you should never touch a strange dog.

If Erik actually were a strange dog, I'd hold out my hand for him to sniff. So that's what I did. Except since he's a boy, I kept my palm up and made sure there was chocolate inside. "Here. Try one of these."

"What's this?" he asked.

"Amazing Swiss chocolate. It's imported." I didn't really know what this meant, but Dweeble had said it like it was something impressive.

"What are you doing, trying to bribe me?" he asked.

"No." I shook my head.

Erik scoffed. "You can't ask me to give up our lunch spot for some chocolate."

"I know. I'm not. Seriously. It doesn't even matter that we've been sitting there since day one, or that you guys don't need all that room. Or that all we want is less than half the table. I don't care. I just thought you might like this."

He took the chocolate like he was doing me some huge favor.

"We'll sit somewhere else," I told him. "It's not a big deal, so don't even worry about it. Okay? It's cool. We don't really like that spot, anyway." I turned around to go.

"Hey, Spaz," he called.

"I don't respond to that."

"Okay, whatever your name is."

I spun around and looked him straight in the eye. "I'm Annabelle. You know that." Then I headed back over to my friends, walking tall, in case he was still watching. Sure I'd lost, but at least I'd tried.

"What was that about?" asked Rachel.

"Nothing," I replied.

Emma stared at me. "No, you did something just then."

I tucked my hair behind my ears and looked away. "I just gave Erik some chocolate."

"Why'd you do that? He's such a jerk," said Rachel.

"Was it so he'd move?" asked Claire.

"Not exactly. Well, kind of. Maybe we should just eat by the trash cans? It's only one lunch. Tomorrow, I'll try and get here first."

"Hey, look," said Rachel, pointing to the lunch table.

I turned around to find Erik and Joe and the other

two Corn Dog Boys moving their backpacks out of the way. A second later they slid over to make room for us.

It was a miracle!

Okay, not quite. But my plan had worked, which was very cool.

We hurried over and claimed our spot. We had to squish so all five of us would fit, but what did I care? We didn't get stuck eating by the trash!

After lunch, as we were packing up, I thanked Erik for giving us space, because dogs need positive reinforcement. My friends thought I was weird for doing it, and they were probably right, but I figured it was better to be safe than stuck eating with the flies.

chapter eleven
scaredy-cats

Phys Ed still annoyed me, and not because I got picked last for basketball. Yes, that bruised my ego, but I would've gotten over it had I actually been able to play in the game.

Our teams are coed, but usually the boys hog the ball the whole time. A few girls try and get in on the game, but most would rather stand around and talk on the sidelines. I've tried playing every day but no one would pass to me. Not even when I was wide open.

Today I got sick and tired of waiting around, so I stole the ball from Tommy St. James in the third quarter. As I dribbled down the court, he called me "Spaz," and started yelling about how I'd fouled him, but that was a lie, and no one listened to him, anyway. Everyone on his team was too busy trying to get the ball back, but no one could.

I faked left and right, leaving them all in the dust. Once I made it to the top of the key, I sped in for a layup, and shot. The ball swooshed through the net, without even hitting the rim.

My team cheered so loud it drowned out Tommy's whining. I stole the ball again a few minutes later and then I finally got passed to. I scored twice more, and we ended up winning the game by four points.

Afterward Sanjay, the team captain, high fived me and said, "That was awesome. You're on a roll, Annabelle." Yeah, that's right. A boy actually called me by my real name *and* he was nice to me.

"Um, thanks," I said, shrugging and grinning and probably blushing. What else could I say? It was true. And he didn't even know the half of it.

Everything would have been so perfect had my day ended right then, but as I was on my way to the parking lot to meet my mom, I realized I'd forgotten my math book. I turned around and headed back to the locker area.

School's-over excitement buzzed through the air. Doors clanged, kids rushed by, talking, laughing, yelling, and even squealing. One boy tried to shove his friend into me, but I scrambled away just in time.

When I got close to my locker, I noticed some guy leaning against it.

Figuring I could handle the situation, I didn't freak out. But that was before I realized it was Jackson.

His left shoulder pressed into the grate—my locker grate—as he talked to some other guy, five lockers down. The two of them took up so much space, like they owned the whole school. I waited for a minute, hoping Jackson's friend would get what he needed, so they could both just move on. But the guy took forever.

I soon lost patience. Jackson was just a boy. And boys were dogs. I'd already trained a bunch.

Okay I'd trained a few. Temporarily. Still, I told myself I had nothing to fear. Jackson was no different. And now I knew what to do.

Taking a deep breath, I said, "Excuse me."

Either he didn't hear me, or he pretended not to.

I tried again, louder this time. "Hey, Jackson?"

He glanced over his shoulder, smirked, and then turned back to his friend like I didn't even matter.

By now, the halls were emptying out. I knew my mom was waiting. "I need to get in there," I said, but he ignored me.

Jackson's friend slammed his locker shut, said, "See you, dude," and took off.

I thought Jackson would leave too, but he didn't. Instead, he leaned back on my locker, with his legs crossed in front of him. He looked too comfortable. Happy even. Like bugging me was some great new sport and he was desperate to play first string.

Some kid zipped by on a skateboard, even though they were banned from campus, along with sneaker skates and razor scooters. He came inches from mowing us down.

Jackson didn't flinch.

I tried not to, but felt my jaw tremble.

Now we were all alone.

He stared at me and I stared at my sneakers.

My mom would be wondering where I was.

I repeated my boy-training lessons in my head.

Be the dominant one. Speak firmly. Look him in the eye. Don't ask. Order.

If I were facing anyone else, this would've been easy. These past couple of weeks had been going so well. At least that's what I told myself.

The problem was, Jackson seemed like an entirely different animal. Maybe it was because he was an eighth grader. *You can't teach an old dog new tricks.* I didn't read that in my dog-training book, but it's one of those things people say all the time, so maybe it's true.

Still, I had to at least try. My voice wavered even though I struggled to speak steadily. "Come on, Jackson. Just move."

He smiled a slow, drawn-out smile. Then he stretched his arms over his head, like he was just waking up or something. "But it's so comfortable here."

"I need to get my stuff."

"What's your hurry?" Jackson yawned, but I could tell he was faking.

"My mom is waiting. I don't want to be late."

"You've been late before and you survived."

I'd like to do more than survive here, I thought but didn't say. I didn't know how to answer him so I didn't speak. I couldn't even look at him.

Maybe I didn't really need my math book. Maybe I could just do my homework in the morning, before class. No, that wouldn't work.

Remembering how well the chocolate had worked on other boys, I pulled the last piece out of my bag and offered it to Jackson. "Um, here. This is for you."

"What?" He spoke sharply.

But before I could answer, he'd grabbed it out of my hand. He looked from it to me and laughed a mean laugh.

"You've got to be kidding me."

Okay, bad move. Really bad move. The chocolate seemed measly. Weak. Sad, even. Just like me. But it was too late. I'd come too far, and I couldn't turn back. "It's imported?" Pathetic, I know, but what else could I say?

"Well, this looks fantastic. Thank you, Spama-belle." Jackson twisted his face into a mean sneer. Then he unwrapped the chocolate, turned around, and smashed it against my lock.

I gasped. He'd wasted my last piece. He'd caked my lock in delicious Swiss chocolate. Except it didn't look like chocolate anymore. . . .

Jackson watched me, amused. He was actually enjoying this. Finally he walked away, calling over his shoulder, "All you had to do was say please."

Yeah, right.

Once I was sure he wasn't coming back, I dug a tissue out of my backpack, and cleaned off the lock. I couldn't get all the chocolate out of the crack around the dial, but did the best I could. It took me three tries to open up my locker. My hands shook so much, I kept messing up and passing the right numbers.

And once I did get my math book, I left brown fingerprints all over it.

As soon as I got home, I consulted my book.

❧Taming the Unruly Dog: Scaredy-Cats Stay Back❧

Never show fear. People show fear in subtle ways, and dogs are very perceptive. A dog that knows you're scared is never going to listen to you. So buck up. Dog training is about attitude. Namely, you should have one. If you don't have one, you need to find one. If you can't do that, pretend that you do. Act like you're calm, confident, and in control, and your dog will listen to you.

So easy to read. So hard to do. Obviously Jackson knew I was scared of him. How can you hide something like that?

You can't.

Which is why I needed a new plan.

From now on, I'd spend the rest of sixth grade avoiding Jackson.

chapter twelve
buttons breaks and laundry aches

That night, while I was reading over the final draft of my book report, Pepper jumped onto my bed. "Down, boy," I said.

He ignored me. Probably because he was too busy barking at Buttons, my stuffed hippo. Gran gave me Buttons when I was born. She's fat and blue with blond braids and red shoes. (The hippo, I mean. Not Gran.) She used to have matching buttons running down her front but they all fell off. I know I'm too old to have stuffed animals, but Buttons is too cute and raggedy to give up. This made it really annoying when Pepper grabbed her by the hair, jumped off the bed, and fled.

Yesterday, he'd taken one of Dweeble's running shoes and tried to bury it behind the tomato plants. Fearing my hippo would soon share the same fate, I chased Pepper downstairs and through the kitchen, finally cornering him in the dining room.

"Drop it," I said. It was like he didn't even hear me. He tried to run past me but I managed to grab ahold of Buttons's foot. I tried yanking her away, but that just made him grip her even tighter.

It didn't matter how hard I pulled. He wouldn't let go. "Come on. Drop it. Please drop it, Pepper."

His teeth sunk deeper into her fur. His lips curled up, exposing his pink gums. Gums I used to find adorable.

"Let go, Pepper!"

I gave it a sharp tug and finally managed to rip Buttons from Pepper. But not all of her. Buttons's hair and half her head were still in Pepper's mouth. I stared at Buttons's bottom half, horrified.

"You just scalped my favorite stuffed animal!"

Pepper's tail wagged.

I held Buttons up to his face. Cotton stuffing puffed from the top of her head. "Her brains are oozing out. You murdered Buttons."

Pepper dropped Buttons's head-half to try and get the rest of her. Obviously the gravity of the situation was lost on him.

Once I had both pieces out of his reach, I led him into the backyard, and left him there, so I could take a look at the dog-training book.

☙ THE FUN IS IN THE CHASE, SO DON'T DO IT ☙

If your dog has something of yours that he shouldn't, whatever you do, DON'T CHASE. He'll think it's a game. Instead, ignore him. If that doesn't work, then distract him with something else.

Eventually, he'll lose interest. It may take awhile, but it's worth the wait. Seriously. This works.

I went outside with my already ruined sandal and a pocket full of dog biscuits to try it out.

Pepper grabbed the sandal as soon as he saw it. He preferred shoes, socks, and pillows to the actual toys we bought for him. If it wasn't so destructive, it might be cute.

Once I held up a dog biscuit and said, "Drop it!" he let go of the sandal and went for the treat instead.

"Good boy," I said, grabbing the sandal. "Now let's try it again."

I gave him back the sandal. "Now drop it," I said, offering him another treat. "Nice work, Pepper!"

We practiced for a while.

When I headed back inside I found my mom digging through her purse, probably in search of her keys. "Want to come to the grocery store with me, Annabelle?"

"No thanks."

"Then can you do me a favor? I didn't manage to finish the laundry. There's a load in the dryer now. Will you fold everything after it's ready?"

"Why can't Ted do it?"

"He's working late, and he's leaving for Switzerland in just two days. He's got a lot to take care of."

I sighed like it pained me. "Do I have to?"

"You don't have to, but you'd be doing me a huge favor," Mom said.

Yup, I had to. "Okay, fine."

"Thank you." She squeezed my arm before heading out the door.

Pepper and I headed upstairs, so I could do more homework and he could nap at my feet.

The dinging of the dryer woke him up twenty minutes later.

Pepper's ears perked up and he let out a low growl.

"It's okay, Pep," I said.

He followed me downstairs to the garage, where I began unloading the clean clothes.

It wasn't fun, exactly, but it did seem cool, having a washing machine and a dryer in our house. We didn't have one in the old apartment, which meant that Mom had to go to the Laundromat every Saturday morning. If I didn't have other plans, she'd make me come along. It was boring being there, cooped up inside. The machines were too loud to have a conversation over and the chairs weren't comfortable to sit in. For a while, Mom and I would drop our stuff in the wash and then head to the diner across the street for breakfast. But one day someone stole our sheets. So after that, we had to stay inside and guard everything.

Now if I needed clean clothes, I didn't have to wait until the weekend. I could have them anytime.

I dumped our dry clothes into a white plastic basket and headed for the living room to fold. Everything was still warm and it smelled good. Not as good as an ocean breeze, like the fabric softener had promised. But good, just the same.

I took the dish towels right to the kitchen, folded them carefully and put them in the drawer next to the silverware. Then I folded my two new T-shirts— the ones that Pepper hadn't destroyed. Luckily, they were already soft and worn looking—in a good way, not in an old way.

As much as I missed St. Catherine's and the ease of not having to deal with dumb boys five days a week, I had to admit, it was nice wearing whatever I wanted to at school.

It was also fun seeing how certain kids wore clothes that matched their personalities. Emma always looked neat and tucked in. Yumi dressed like she was going to or coming from a baseball game. And Claire is kind of a hippy, who makes her own tie-dyes and even embroiders flowers and peace signs onto her jeans. It was much cooler than being surrounded by girls in plaid every single day.

I was almost done with the folding when I spotted something horrifying at the bottom of the basket.

Dweeble's running shorts.

I stared down at them for a while, afraid to get too close. So big and loud and bright, they seemed out of place among my and mom's clothes. I wondered if I could just put the basket away, back in the garage, and pretend like I hadn't noticed. But they were Oompa Loompa orange. There's no way they could be missed.

I carefully picked them up by the drawstring, using only my thumb and forefinger. Eew. I cringed. I couldn't help myself. These were shorts he'd sweated in. Yes, they were clean now, but there was still something icky about it. Worse, something gray flapped around inside the lining.

They had underwear already sewn in.

I dropped the shorts faster than a hot potato—shocked that Mom had asked me to fold Dweeble's underwear. And worse, Dweeble's underwear and mine had tumbled around together in the same dryer. Like they all belonged together, which they so clearly didn't.

The shorts lay in a crumpled heap on the floor. I wanted to pick them up, like it was no big deal, but I couldn't do it. Instead, I tipped the basket to its side and kicked Dweeble's shorts back in. Then I threw Mom's stuff on top and left the entire basket outside the door to their room.

chapter thirteen
cut to the chase

I got to Birchwood early on Friday and didn't even dread being there. Campus was so quiet it seemed peaceful.

After a quick trip to my locker, I sat down on an empty bench in the West Quad and pulled out my book report. I wanted to read it one last time before turning it in. Sure, it sounds nerdy, but there's something exciting about handing over an assignment you've worked hard on, when you're pretty sure you're going to get a good grade.

Thanks to Tobias, Mr. Beller thought I was a nuisance. I looked forward to proving to him that I wasn't some dumb kid who disrupted class on purpose. I was just an innocent victim, someone fully capable of doing well. I hoped.

But after I pulled the report out of my backpack, before I even read the opening sentence, it disappeared.

Yup, that's right. My report was gone.

Someone ripped the pages right out of my hands.

By the time I realized what'd happened, Erik was halfway to the locker bank. "This yours?" he asked, carelessly waving my report by the spine. Dumb question, but I was in no position to criticize.

"Give it back." When I jumped up and went after him, he turned and ran.

I chased him, of course, but I couldn't keep up. Erik had a big head start. Plus, my backpack slowed me down.

"Come on, Erik," I yelled.

He held my report in one fist. As his arms pumped back and forth, the pages flapped around. I knew they'd be wrinkled by the time I got them back. If I got them back.

I chased Erik through the locker banks, all around the East Quad and into the cafeteria. Erik weaved through tables and around kids. Some watched us, but most were too focused on their bagels and muffins to notice the commotion.

Finally, I managed to jump over an empty bench and corner him at the snack machine. Out of breath, his eyes darted around in search of an escape. He held my report behind his back. With his body pressed up against the wall, there wasn't room to reach around and grab it.

"Dude, what's up?" asked Tobias, who'd just strolled up behind me with a half eaten donut in his hand.

"Don't know. This chick is chasing me," said Erik.

No one had ever called me a chick before and I didn't like it. A chick is a baby chicken—cute and fluffy but totally helpless. Erik had basically called me a baby.

"I'm not chasing you. I'm chasing my book report. Give it back." I didn't ask him. I told him. My tone was strong and commanding, but for once it didn't do me any good. Maybe because I was facing two dominant dogs.

"SPAZ!" Erik yelled in my face and spittle landed on my cheek. Nasty! As I wiped it away he darted around the table. I tried running after him, but Tobias grabbed my backpack, which was still attached to my back. So I didn't get very far. But neither did Erik, because I snagged his T-shirt.

"Hey, let me go," he yelled.

But I wouldn't. "I need that." I lunged for the pages with my free hand.

He held it just out of reach. "You're stretching out my shirt."

"You're messing up my report."

"Okay, fine, fine. If you let go of me I'll give you your stupid homework."

"It's not stupid," I said, relaxing my hold.

Tobias let go of my bag.

Erik held out my book report, but as soon as I reached for it, he tossed it to Tobias.

Except he missed, so my report landed on the ground. When I bent down to get it, Tobias did, too and we bumped heads.

"Ow!" I yelled, clutching my forehead. He'd really clocked me. My whole head throbbed.

Worse, Tobias recovered first and grabbed my report.

He took off with it and I chased after him. Twice, I grazed the pages with my fingertips, but couldn't get close enough to grab it.

Erik waved his hands. "Over here."

Tobias tossed my report like a Frisbee. The pages flapped in the breeze. Erik caught it and tucked it under his arm. It was hopeless. They were actually laughing. This was fun for them.

What if they destroyed my report like Pepper had destroyed Buttons?

Suddenly it hit me.

When your dog has something of yours, don't chase him. He'll think it's a game. Instead, ignore him. Eventually, he'll lose interest.

I stopped in my tracks.

Erik kept running. He turned the corner at the end of the locker banks and disappeared.

As hard as it was, I let him go.

Instead of following him, I headed straight for the bench where I'd been sitting when my report was stolen.

I sat down and waited, hoping they'd lose interest, because chasing them wasn't working and I didn't know what else to do.

Except blink hard to keep my tears from falling.

And try not to think about how awful everything was right now.

Or about how this never would've happened at St. Catherine's.

The first bell rang. I stayed where I was for a minute, but with no sign of Erik or Tobias, I figured I should head to class. Better to show up empty-handed than empty-handed and late. I still had everything saved on my computer at home. Maybe Mr. Beller would let me turn it in on Monday. Probably not, though. He'd been warning us about his "no excuses, no extensions" policy all week.

The worst part about this mess was that when I showed up without my report, Mr. Beller wouldn't even be surprised. He already thought I was trouble—and all for reasons that weren't my fault. I didn't even know how to get him to change his mind. I'd never had to deal with a teacher not liking me. Teachers *always* liked me. At least they used to.

I circled the building a few times, trying to come up with a decent excuse.

I didn't know the report was due today.

I left it at home.

My dog ate it.

Nothing seemed good enough. I was out of ideas, and the final bell was about to ring, so I walked into the room.

Everyone else had their reports out on their desks and ready to hand in. Even Tobias.

I tried to ignore him, but as soon as I sat down, he kicked me.

Oh, great. That again. "Stop it," I whispered.

He didn't.

It was like the past two weeks had never happened. He kept on kicking. I was out of chocolate, and too upset to scold him.

Then another passage from the book flashed to mind.

Your name is Pete and Repeat is your game. In other words, dogs have short memories, which is why you need to reinforce their training, giving them the same lessons over and over and over again.

Did that mean I'd have to go through this nearly every single day for the rest of my life? Or was it just Tobias with the short-term memory? What about the rest of the boys? It was all so much work.

Tobias kicked me harder so I whipped my head around and shot him a dirty look. His glasses were on crooked but I didn't bother telling him. "Cut it out," I said.

"You're no fun, Spaz," he replied, and handed over my book report.

I grabbed it, turned around, and flipped through the wrinkled pages. It smelled like the cafeteria. I cringed at the ketchup stain on the back cover. Page four had a tear down the middle, but if you lined up the two pieces, you could still read everything. I raised my hand and asked Mr. Beller for some tape. He gave me a suspicious look, but still motioned for me to come up to his desk and then pushed the tape dispenser toward me.

"Thank you," I said, taking two pieces back to my desk. I stuck the pages back together. It wasn't pretty, but at least it was readable.

I sat back, marveling over how the dog/boy training book had worked for me, yet again.

Then something occurred to me. If Tobias were an actual dog, I'd have said, "Good boy," and patted him on his head. So, taking a deep breath, I turned around and put on my best fake smile. "Thank you so much, Tobias. It was so sweet of you to bring it back."

"Whatever," Tobias grumbled.

"And please thank Erik for me, too."

It wasn't easy, thanking the boys for giving me back what was rightfully mine. But I always gave Pepper positive reinforcement.

Hmm. Maybe if I got Jackson a really delicious chew toy, he'd leave me alone.

chapter fourteen
jackson strikes again

On Friday night, the doorbell rang, which always drives Pepper crazy. It's like there's some invisible wire connecting the button to his brain, or maybe it's just the sound. He hears it and goes nuts, running straight for the front of the house, barking his head off and jumping up and down in front of the door like there's a lifetime supply of dog biscuits on the other side of it. Or maybe he's trying to push the entire thing open himself, with some combination of his front paws and the sheer weight of his excitement. I guess the concepts of locks and doorknobs are pretty much beyond his grasp.

"I'll get it," I yelled, running downstairs.

Mom sat in the living room, grading papers. Dweeble was on the floor, waxing his skis. Big shocker—they were gigantic and fluorescent yellow.

"The little guy is turning into quite the guard dog," said Mom.

I had to laugh. "Some guard dog. If anyone tries to break in, he'll lick them to death."

"Well at least he can protect us against burglars who are allergic to dogs," Dweeble added.

"Hey, that's funny," I said, as I headed to the entryway.

"Don't sound so surprised," Dweeble replied.

I used one hand to hold Pepper's collar and the other to open up the door.

Mia and Sophia stood on the front step, sleeping bags tucked under their arms and backpacks strapped to their backs.

"You're here!" I yelled.

Sure, it had only been a few weeks since we said good-bye after camp, but it seemed like months. And going by the way they screamed, "Annabelle!" I'm pretty sure they felt the same way.

"Come in," I said.

Once the door was safely shut, I let go of the dog and hugged them.

Pepper jumped and almost knocked over Sophia, but she didn't mind. "He's the cutest!" She bent down so Pepper could lick her face.

"Oh, but his breath stinks," she added, scrunching up her nose.

It wasn't something I could really argue with, but it seemed weird to bring it up first thing. Of course, that was Sophia.

"He's adorable, Annabelle. I want a dog," Mia cooed.

"You already have a turtle and a gerbil," said Sophia. "If anyone gets a new pet, it should be me."

"The turtle is my sister's and he's pretty boring," said Mia.

I took them upstairs so they could drop their stuff off in my room. Pepper ran ahead. When he got to the top of the steps, he turned around and ran back down, I guess to make sure we were still coming. Sophia almost tripped over him, but I grabbed her arm and steadied her at the last second.

Once we were in my room, Mia looked around. "This place is huge," she said.

"My cousins' house is bigger, and they have a pool," Sophia said. She headed to my window and looked out. "You do have a nice view of the street, though."

"Hi, girls." My mom came in, asking, "Has Annabelle offered to give you the grand tour yet?"

"We're too busy," I told her. House tours were boring and I'm surprised my mom didn't know any better.

"Well, make yourselves at home," she said.

"Do you have any Pop Tarts?" asked Sophia.

Mom seemed confused. "Ah, no. I don't think so."

"Well, how can I make myself at home if there aren't any Pop Tarts? We always have Pop Tarts at my house." Sophia has a weird sense of humor. The kind that isn't always funny. (But at least she'd finally stopped telling knock-knock jokes.)

We all knew to ignore her. Even my mom, who said, "Okay, then. I'll leave you girls alone, now."

As she ducked out of my room, Mia asked, "Can we take your dog for a walk?"

"Sure," I said, and we headed back downstairs for Pepper's leash.

Once we got outside, Sophia said, "Let me hold him, okay?"

Mia and I looked at each other and smiled. This was typical Sophia, always wanting to be in charge.

"He's kind of wild," I said. "I should start out, but you can hold the leash later on."

She opened her mouth to argue but then changed her mind, and looked at her nails, instead. They were painted purple, and so were Mia's.

Mia and Sophia did stuff like that all the time— painting their nails the same color and wearing their hair in matching styles. Sometimes they even dressed alike, which was funny because they looked and acted like opposites. They both have long dark hair, but Sophia is short and chubby, with big blue eyes and lots of freckles. And Mia is skinny, with brown eyes and no freckles. She towers over both of us, but she's so quiet, I usually forget she's so tall.

Anyway, today I noticed it wasn't just their nails that matched. They also wore identical cowboy boots. They were tan, with a pink embroidered flower on the pointy toe. "When did you get those?" I asked.

"My mom took us to the mall last Sunday," said Mia.

"I thought your mom's car was in the shop," I said.

"It was. She got it out that morning."

"Oh."

"I asked her to take us to your house, but she said it was too far," said Mia.

"But at least we're here now," Sophia added.

This was true. And anyway, I never wanted to dress alike the way they did, especially since we'd had to wear uniforms at school every day. Sophia and Mia knew this, but they usually asked me if I wanted to get their same shoes and clothes or whatever. It seemed strange that they didn't ask this time, but I guess that's what I get for moving away. Not that it was my choice or anything.

As we walked to the end of the cul-de-sac, Mia's and Sophia's boots click-clacked along the sidewalk. Even their steps matched, a constant reminder that I was no longer a part of their regular life. I tried not to think about it.

Once we were off my street, I showed them all of Pepper's new tricks. He sat when I told him to sit. He raised his paw when I told him to shake. He walked by my side when I told him to heel. Well, except for when he tried to chase after a squirrel.

Once I got him to calm down, Sophia asked, "Can I hold Pepper now?"

"Sure." I handed over the leash, and showed her how to put it on properly. "Make sure your wrist goes through the loop, and hold the leash in the palm of your hand. If you hold it with your fingers, you might break one."

"Okay," said Sophia.

"And make sure you don't let go. He gets really

hyper when cars goes by. I'm trying to train him not to chase them, but so far, it hasn't worked."

"I'll be careful," Sophia promised.

"Oh, and try to steer clear of garbage cans. He loves eating trash. Last Wednesday I wasn't paying attention and he knocked one over and tried to eat a moldy piece of pizza. It's not easy prying stuff from his mouth."

"Okay, already." Sophia started walking forward but Pepper stopped in his tracks and looked up at me with his adorable big eyes.

I bent over and gave him a quick scratch behind his ears. "It's okay," I told him. "Just be good."

"You talk to him?" Mia asked.

I shrugged. "Sometimes."

"So what's your new school like?" asked Mia. "Do you like it?"

"It's okay," I said. This wasn't a total lie. Birchwood was great when I hung out with Rachel and her friends, and terrible when I got stuck with boys like Tobias and Erik. Add those different experiences together and divide, and you come up with okay. (Jackson brought the average way down, but since I'd successfully avoided him since the locker incident, I didn't factor him into the equation.)

Of course, Birchwood was the last thing I wanted to think about, so I changed the subject. "What's happening at St. Catherine's?"

"Not much." Mia shrugged.

"Half of the fifth graders went home yesterday

with head lice," said Sophia. "And there's a new sixth grade math teacher."

"She's nice, but she gives too much homework," said Mia.

"It was Sara's birthday yesterday and she brought in donuts with rainbow sprinkles," said Sophia. "I told her chocolate would've been better, and she acted all offended. I don't know why. I just thought it would be a good tip, you know, for next year."

It was getting dark, so we turned around and headed back. As soon as we got to my street, I noticed that Rachel and Jackson's garage door was open. I could hear someone moving around inside. Fearing the worst, I stopped short.

"Hey, guys? Let's cross the street now." I tried to sound casual about it, but clearly my voice sounded funny. My friends glanced at me like they knew something was up.

"What's the hurry?" asked Sophia.

"Um, my friend Rachel is allergic," I said, pointing to her house. "And I don't want her having an attack." I felt bad for making up fake excuses (even though it was based on the truth), but the real reason I was avoiding the house seemed too embarrassing to explain. How could I tell my friends I was nervous around some dumb boy? And I didn't even know if Jackson was in there. It could've been anyone— Rachel, their mom, the exterminator—which meant that basically I was afraid of the *possibility* of a boy. You can't get much more pathetic than that.

"So Pepper can't even walk on her sidewalk?" asked Sophia. "You know that's public property. She can't make you stay away."

"She doesn't make me. It's just—"

"Hey, Spazabelle!" Jackson yelled.

Uh-oh.

Jackson walked out of the garage and stood in the middle of his driveway, with his skateboard tucked under his arm.

Mia gasped and grabbed my arm. "Who's that cute boy?" she whispered.

"Ew! No one." I jumped off the sidewalk and headed across the street, getting as far away from him as possible. "Let's go," I said, motioning to my friends.

They followed me until Jackson called, "Whatcha doin', Spaz?"

Then Sophia stopped in her tracks and glanced over her shoulder. "What did he call you?"

"Nothing." I grabbed her arm and pulled her away. "Come on!"

"It's the Spazerator. Walking her dumb dog," he called.

"But who is he?" she asked.

"He's just my friend Rachel's older brother. He's kind of a jerk."

"You go to school with him?" asked Mia.

"Unfortunately."

"But what did he just call you?" asked Sophia.

"Will you please drop it?" I walked inside and trudged up to my room.

"He's cute," said Mia.

"You already said that."

"Super-cute," Sophia said, and they both giggled.

Jackson makes fun of me in front of my friends, and they think he's cute? Ouch. "He's really annoying."

"You can be cute and annoying at the same time," said Sophia.

"But Jackson's so annoying, it cancels out his cuteness," I insisted. "Believe me. I've given this a lot of thought."

"Okay, fine. But he's just one boy. What about the rest of them? You must like someone," said Sophia.

Just thinking about the Birchwood boys, and Jackson especially, made me feel sick to my stomach. "Will you stop asking me that."

"Well, you don't have to get mad," said Sophia.

"I can't help it," I said, fuming now. "You won't leave me alone and you just don't get it. Going to school with boys isn't what you think it is. It's not like in the movies, where they're all sweet, texting girls and buying them flowers and opening doors and stuff."

"You don't have to yell," said Sophia.

"I'm not yelling," I yelled.

We both looked at Mia, who shrugged. This could have meant, "I don't know," or, "I'm not taking sides."

Neither answer would've helped. I took a deep breath and turned back to Sophia. "I'm just trying to explain."

"Well, then explain. What's it like?" asked Sophia.

"Remember the camp dance? Boys are like that, but a hundred times worse. It's like going to school with a bunch of wild dogs."

Mia and Sophia looked at each other and cracked up.

"Seriously, you guys."

The more I insisted, the harder they laughed. There wasn't any way to get them to understand. Mia and Sophia looked like my best friends and sounded like my best friends, but something had changed between us. And whatever it was, I didn't like it. Usually our sleepovers flew by. Now it was only eight o'clock and we'd already run out of things to talk about.

"I miss St. Catherine's," I said, once they finally calmed down. "I wish I could go back."

"Me, too," said Mia. "We really miss you."

Sophia seemed confused. "Don't get me wrong. I wish you could come back, too. But I don't get why you'd want to. You live in this really cool house, and you have a dog, and St. Catherine's is so boring."

I opened my mouth, all set to try and explain, but there wasn't any way to make her understand. St. Catherine's didn't seem boring to me. But even if that were the case, I'd have preferred boring to the torture-inducing experience known as Birchwood Middle School.

chapter fifteen
dweeble takes flight

Dweeble made us waffles and hot cocoa in the morning, before Mia and Sophia got picked up.

Then he spent the rest of the day packing. He was flying to Switzerland that night, and boy, were his arms going to be tired. Yeah, he actually made that joke. Even worse, since no one laughed the first time, he tried it again an hour later. Mom giggled on try number two, probably because she felt sorry for him.

I could've told him that joke wasn't ever going to be funny, but decided not to. It wasn't Dweeble's fault he was humor-challenged. And at least he tried. I guess I was feeling pretty generous, since he'd be gone for an entire week. I even hugged him good-bye.

"Do you want anything from Switzerland?" he asked.

"Um, maybe some more of that chocolate?"

Dweeble grinned. "I noticed that went quickly."

"Sorry," I said.

"Don't be. It was there to be eaten. Here's the thing, though." Dweeble winked at my mom. "I can get the chocolate here, which makes me think, maybe I don't really need to go."

I could tell this was another one of his bad jokes, but the thought still scared me.

"Your bags are already in the car, so you may as well," Mom said, linking her arm through his and dragging him to the door. "Plus, Jason is expecting you."

"Yes, those are excellent points. And I can see you both want to get rid of me." Dweeble waved good-bye. "I'll see you next week, Annabelle."

"Bye. Have fun. Tell Jason I say hello."

I worried that was a weird thing to say, since Jason and I didn't even know each other, but Dweeble grinned and said, "I will." So maybe it wasn't so wrong.

"Are you sure you don't want to come to the airport with us?" asked my mom.

Like I wanted to witness their sappy good-bye? I don't think so. "No, thanks."

"I'll be home in two hours, max. Hopefully sooner." Mom seemed nervous about leaving me in the house alone. Did I need to remind her that I was already eleven years old?

"I'll be fine," I told her.

As their car pulled out of the driveway, I had to smile. With Dweeble in Switzerland, it meant I'd have seven whole days free of corny jokes. There wouldn't be any waiting for Dweeble to go running before we could eat dinner. Nor would I have to put up with his lousy music.

Once they were gone, I tried calling Rachel. When Jackson answered, I panicked and hung up, fast.

Then I went up to my room because I promised to clean it before my mom got back. Pepper came too. I brought one of his chew toys with me, so he wouldn't try eating any of my stuff.

But before I even finished making my bed, the phone rang.

I ran to my desk and picked it up. "Hello?"

"Who's this?" asked a familiar-sounding boy's voice.

I replied without thinking. "Annabelle. Who's this?"

Instead of answering me he asked, "Why are you crank calling our house, Spazabelle?"

Jackson! Ack! How did he know? And what do I do? Could I hang up? I couldn't just hang up. I had to say something. But what?

I coughed. "I'm not. I didn't. Um, what are you talking about?"

"I'm talking about caller ID. We have it. And you just cranked us. So what gives?"

Squeezing my eyes shut tight, I wished this wasn't happening. I had to say something. I could hear him breathing on the other end of the line. "Is Rachel there?"

"Maybe."

"Can I talk to her?"

"She's going to be mad when she hears you called and hung up."

"I didn't mean to do it."

"You're saying you *accidentally* hung up on me?"

Okay, time to switch tactics. "Was that you on the phone?" I asked innocently. "I thought I dialed wrong so I hung up."

He didn't say anything, which tripped me up even more.

"Um, the phone must've slipped, I think."

"You think?" he spat out.

I cringed. I was making things worse. I knew I was but I couldn't help myself. Talking to Jackson got me all flustered. I wasn't prepared for this. And I couldn't be, either. It's not like Pepper talked on the phone. No dog-training lessons applied. I was on my own here.

On my own and floundering.

"Why do you want to talk to my dumb sister, anyway?" He sounded so nasty. Sinister, even—like a cartoon villain.

"Just put her on the phone, please."

"So you agree that my sister is dumb?"

"Wait. What? No, I never said that."

"Hey, Rachel," Jackson yelled. "Annabelle just called you dumb."

Sure, now he calls me by my real name. "Cut it out," I yelled. My hand gripped the phone tighter. "You know I never said that. Tell Rachel I never said that."

"Geez, will you chill? She's not even home."

He hung up on me.

I sat there for a few moments, with the dial tone ringing in my ear. What if Jackson told Rachel I'd crank called their house? What if he told her I said she was dumb?

I wondered if I should go wait for her outside so I could explain the whole thing before Jackson got the chance to. But how could I explain? The truth was too embarrassing. Anyway, who knew when she'd be home? Maybe Jackson was lying anyway and she was home and they were both laughing at me this very second. Okay, I didn't think Rachel would actually laugh at me, but she'd have to think I was a little weird for calling and hanging up.

I didn't know what to do. But sitting in my room was making me worry like crazy, so I took Pepper for a walk. As soon as we made it to the sidewalk, I feared Jackson might come outside, so I ran past his house. The good news: he didn't. The bad news: running away made me feel like a big, fat wimp.

By the time I got home, my mom was back.

"Hi," I called.

"Oh, there you are," she said, as she walked into the entryway, all smiley.

"Are you that excited that your boyfriend is leaving the country?" I meant for it to be a joke, but it came out sounding kind of mean, so I added, "I'm kidding."

She didn't even seem that upset. "I'm just excited about our week together. And I have a surprise for you."

"What?" I asked.

"Come see." She waved me inside, and told me before I had time to figure it out. "I brought home dinner from Hunan Park."

Hunan Park is our favorite Chinese restaurant. They don't deliver as far as Westlake, obviously, so we hadn't had it since before summer. I followed her into the kitchen, where the familiar smells of moo shu pork and vegetable lo mein wafted from two takeout bags on the counter. Yum.

I walked over to the cabinet next to the sink and pulled out a couple of place mats.

"What are you doing?" asked Mom.

"Setting the kitchen table."

"Just get plates and napkins. We'll eat in the living room."

I turned around, surprised. "But the coffee table is from France."

Mom let out a laugh. "Oh, lots of things are from France, honey. That doesn't mean they're better than the things from here. And that certainly doesn't mean we can't eat off them."

I wasn't going to argue with that. I piled food onto my plate and grabbed a Sprite. Then Mom and I headed into the living room and settled onto the couch. She grabbed a remote and tried to click on the TV.

"That's the wrong one," I said. Now that we lived with Dweeble, we had six remotes. Different ones operated the cable, the stereo, the DVD player, the surround sound speakers, and I don't know what else, even. I figured out all the important ones right away, but Mom was still pretty much clueless.

"Here you go." I handed her the right remote.

"I don't know why we need so many." She frowned as she turned on the TV.

"Hey, this wasn't my idea."

"I should have rented a movie. Do you want to go get one, later?" Mom balanced her plate in her lap and put her feet on the table.

"We can watch whatever." There's nothing good on Saturday nights, but that wasn't the point. I was happy just hanging out.

She flipped through channels until she came to a National Geographic show about bugs in the rain forest. "This okay?" she asked.

"Sure."

Pepper came over and sniffed our food. He tried eating a dumpling off my plate, but I pulled him away just in time. Then, since he wouldn't leave us alone, I got up and put him in his kennel.

"It's just until we're done eating," I told him.

Pepper barked a bit, but as soon as I walked away, he curled up on his new pillow and closed his eyes.

"You're doing so well with the training," Mom said.

"You haven't seen poor Buttons."

"Your hippo? What happened?"

"She kind of got scalped."

"Oh, Pepper." Mom shook her head. "I'll bring her to the dry cleaners. Maybe they can sew her up. Do you still have the pieces?"

"Yup. That'd be great."

After dinner, Mom made our favorite dessert: popcorn with M&MS mixed in. Then, out of nowhere, she turned off the TV and got all serious, asking, "Are you okay, Annabelle? If there's something going on, or anything you want to talk about . . ."

"What would I want to talk about?"

"Well, last night. Did you have fun with Mia and Sophia? You girls were pretty quiet at breakfast."

"It was fine," I told her, since I didn't know what else to say. Seeing my friends *had* been fun at first. But then Sophia started acting so bossy, and Mia was too quiet. I mean, I guess they were always like that, but it never bothered me before. I don't know what changed.

When Mom didn't say anything I added, "I guess it was kind of weird."

She sighed. "I'm sure Sophia and Mia will always be a part of your life, but it's hard to stay best friends with girls you don't see all the time. Things are so different now, and I know that's hard to accept. But I'm hoping it'll get easier, in time."

I pressed my lips together and didn't respond. Mom stared at me like I was one of those posters with a second, hidden picture inside. She was trying to figure something out, but I didn't know what.

"But you're making new friends, right? Are you happy here? I want to make sure you're happy."

"If I say I don't like it, do we get to move back to

North Hollywood?" I don't know why I asked her this. I knew it would never happen.

"No, but if you're not happy, we'll talk about it and figure out how you can *be* happy."

It was so easy for her to say, when she made all the decisions, and didn't have to deal with Jackson and the other boys from Birchwood Middle School every single day. But I wasn't going to tell her any of that.

"I know it's been a rough couple of weeks, but do you think school might get better?"

I'd never told my mom about my problems at Birchwood, but I guess she could tell. I thought about the boy training I'd already done, and all the training I still had left to do. Dealing with Pepper was easy. Dealing with boys? Not so much. Of course, there was only one Pepper. And there were hundreds of boys.

Maybe I did just need more time.

"It'll be okay, probably," I said.

"I'm sure it will. And just so you know, you're not the only one who misses the old apartment."

"Really?" I asked.

"Of course. It's a big adjustment for me, too. Living in the suburbs, sharing this house. You'll get used to it, though. I promise. Just give it more time. I've been here all summer."

"I guess."

"And you'll get used to living with Ted, too. Don't worry."

I let out a laugh. "I'm not worried about that. Dweeble's completely predictable. All he does is run and cook and listen to lousy music."

Mom stared at me, with her eyebrows wrinkled and her lips pressed together.

"What?" I asked. "I was just kidding. He's a good guy. And I like his cooking."

"But what did you just call him?" she asked, carefully.

Uh-oh. "Um, Weeble. You know how his last name is Weeble?"

Mom didn't say anything at first. My stomach felt funny. All that Chinese food churned from deep within. I shouldn't· have had that third dumpling. Maybe Pepper was trying to tell me something when he tried to steal it off my plate.

Finally, she shook her head slowly ·and said, "I know Ted's last name, and I don't think you called him Weeble, honey."

She was onto me, but I couldn't give it up.

I laughed nervously. "Sure I did. Lots of guys at Birchwood go by their last names. I don't know why. But now I'm used to it." I took a sip of Sprite, just to do something. Maybe it would calm my stomach like ginger ale. Or maybe it was the ginger that did that and not the soda part. "Hey, want to rent that movie now?"

Mom wouldn't let it go. "Funny, because it sounded to me like you said Dweeble. As in, you think my boyfriend is a dweeb."

I tried to keep a straight face, to act like I'd no

idea what she was talking about. "Nope." I shook my head. "You must have misheard me. Which is kind of weird. Is it because you think your boyfriend is a dweeb?"

There was no use trying to get out of it. She knew. I figured she'd scold me or at least ask me to apologize. But instead, she took a swig of her beer, wiped her mouth, and said, "You're very creative, Annabelle."

I reached into the popcorn bowl and took the last few kernels, glancing at her out of the corner of my eye.

Mom bit her bottom lip, looked at me for a second and turned away. Then out of nowhere, she burst into hysterics.

Was she so mad that she'd completely cracked up? I didn't know what was going on until she yelled, "Dweeble!" and then covered her hand with her mouth, because she was laughing so hard.

I smiled at her, hardly believing what was happening. My mother thought it was funny. I didn't want to press my luck, but still said, "You must admit, it kind of fits."

She shook her head back and forth like she knew she shouldn't be laughing but just couldn't help herself. Then she doubled over on the couch and clutched her belly.

Seeing her act like a lunatic made me laugh, too.

"I'm sorry," I squeaked out, which wasn't easy since I was giggling so much.

"No you're not."

"I mean I'm sorry I got caught," I said meekly.

We laughed until it hurt—until we were red faced and out of breath and too exhausted to laugh anymore.

After we calmed down, we sat on the couch in silence, our shoulders touching, dirty plates still stacked on the fancy coffee table. My soda and her beer sat next to them—not on coasters. She put her arm around me and I didn't shrug away.

"So, we're staying here, right?" I asked. "For good?"

"We are, as far as I know." She paused. "Are you okay with that?"

I thought about it for a minute before answering her. I looked around the living room. The puke green carpet didn't look so pukey in the dark. Dweeble wasn't all bad. In fact, he was pretty cool, in his own dweeby way. And it's not like we could move Pepper into an apartment, when he was already used to having a whole backyard.

Jackson was a disaster, but I'd made some progress with Tobias and the other boys. Plus, I still had a few chapters left in the dog-training book. So maybe there was hope.

"It'll be okay," I told her.

I don't know if this was actually true or just wishful thinking. But I wanted it to be true. I wanted it badly.

chapter sixteen
the purple envelope

Rachel called me early the next morning and asked if she could come over.

"Sure," I said.

"Except I'm not allowed to come into your house because of your dog. My mom is afraid I'll have an allergy attack. So can you meet me on your front doorstep?"

"Okay, when?" I asked.

"Right now," she said, like it was obvious.

The doorbell rang before I even hung up. Pepper went crazy-hyper, as usual, barking and jumping and wagging his tail. I tried grabbing him by the collar, but he kept wriggling out of my grasp. I had to struggle to sneak around him, crack the door open the tiniest bit and squeeze through.

"Whew!" I said, once I was safely outside, with the door slammed shut behind me.

Rachel's bike was already parked at the curb, and Rachel herself stood on the front step. She wore another ski cap but this one was gray with blue stripes.

"That was fast," I said.

"I know. I called you from my new cell," she said, holding up a small pink phone.

"Cool!"

"I can only use it for emergencies, but I think this counts." She handed me a purple envelope. "I passed these out at lunch on Friday, but you were already gone."

Right. I'd been ducking out early to go over my boy-training notes. Not that I could actually admit that.

Just then we heard Pepper jump and bark at the door. His nails scraped the wood so hard, he probably left marks. I added that to the ever-growing list of things I had to teach him not to do.

"He's pretty hyper today, huh?" Rachel asked.

"He's like that every day." I wished Pepper didn't have to bark so loud. I flipped the envelope over in my hands. "What's this?" I asked.

"An invitation to my birthday party."

"Cool, thanks. When is it?"

"Well, open it up and find out," Rachel said.

So I did. The invitation was pink, the kind you buy at a fancy stationery store. All Rachel had to do was fill in the date and place and time. She didn't even have to write the words *date*, *place*, or *time* because they were already printed in swirly blue writing.

"Saturday at fourteen minutes past noon," I read.

"That's in six days, not that I'm counting. Okay, that's a lie. I'm totally counting." She looked at her watch. "The party starts in one hundred and forty seven hours and eleven minutes."

"So exact," I said.

"I always start my birthday parties at fourteen minutes past twelve, because that's what time I was born. So can you come?"

At the bottom of the invitation, Rachel had written, "Bring your bathing suit, a beach towel, and a change of clothes," in silver felt-tipped marker.

"We're going to the beach?" I asked.

"No, the party is at my house."

"But you said we should bring beach towels."

Rachel laughed until she realized I was seriously confused.

"I wrote that because beach towels are bigger and softer than regular towels."

"Oh," I said.

"And they're better for lying out," she went on.

"So true," I said, although I'd never laid out before in my entire life. My skin is so pale I have to wear SPF 45 sunblock all summer. Plus, lying around doing nothing is boring. Another problem? Mom and I used the same towels for the bath and the beach. And none of them was particularly big or soft. At least I had some time to figure this all out.

"So who else is going?" I asked.

"The usual crowd. Yumi, Claire, Emma, and you."

"That's it?" I asked.

"That's it. I wanted to invite Miles and Leo from band, but my mom doesn't want too many people at a pool party. She's kind of paranoid sometimes. Plus, she said if I invited boys then Jackson would have to come, too. He's going to a friend's house that day instead. My parents promised."

Even though I was relieved that there wouldn't be any boys (and especially any big brothers) at Rachel's party, I didn't say so. I hadn't realized that Rachel actually had friends who were boys. I didn't want her to know how nervous they made me.

"So can you come? Or do you need to check with your parents first?"

"It's just my mom," I said.

"Really?" asked Rachel. "So who's the bald dude who's always hanging around here?"

"Oh, that's my mom's boyfriend. He lives with us, too."

"Your parents are divorced?" she asked.

"Not exactly."

"So where's your dad?"

No one had asked me that in a while, which was good since the real story is pretty complicated.

I don't have a dad. Not one I've ever met, anyway. Twelve years ago, my mom went to graduate school at Oxford, in England, and came home pregnant with me. My biological father is named Sven Cooper. When he heard the news, he decided he wasn't ready to be a dad. Mom said fine, she didn't need him and neither did I. And we don't.

She told me I shouldn't take this personally because he decided all this before I was even born and he's never met me. They never speak, but she said she'd help me contact him one day if I wanted. Also, if it was okay with him, she'd even take me there to visit. But it was also okay for me never to see him. It was my choice. And so far, I hadn't made up my mind, which I guess meant I was choosing no thanks. At least for now.

But that's a lot to explain to someone. Especially someone I've only known for a few weeks. Even if that person is as cool as Rachel.

"Um, I don't really have a dad," I said, hoping she'd leave it at that.

"Oh," she said. "Hey, what are you doing now?"

I was about to say nothing, but stopped myself. It sounded like Rachel was about to invite me over. And what if Jackson was around? I didn't want to see him on a weekend. Five days a week at school were bad enough. But I couldn't exactly admit that.

"Um, I have a lot of homework," I said, even though I didn't.

"Oh, too bad," said Rachel. "I'm heading over to Yumi's and she told me to invite you, too."

I wanted to tell Rachel I made a mistake, that most of my homework was done, but it was too late. I didn't want her to get suspicious. She'd invited me over twice last week, and I'd had to make up excuses. Pretty soon she might figure out the truth.

"Tell Yumi I say hi," I said glumly.

Rachel was already at the sidewalk. "Will do," she called, before climbing onto her bike and pedaling off.

I watched her cruise down Clemson Court and then disappear around the corner.

It stunk that Rachel was allergic to Pepper. And it stunk even more that I was, well, if not allergic to, then at least extremely repelled by her brother.

chapter seventeen
house arrest

Turned out, there really was a lake in Westlake. Mom finally fixed my squeaky bike and we rode to the lake on Sunday afternoon. We tried riding around it, but some lady in a pink warm-up suit waved us down and explained that the path was for running and walking only.

When we got home, I brushed up on my boy training, and it really paid off. Hardly anyone called me Spam or Spazabelle or any other variation of Annabelle on Monday. In science class, Oliver was nice to me and Tobias ignored me, which was the best I could hope for.

When some boy tried to trip me in the hallway before math, I stepped tall and easily cleared his foot.

A Corn Dog Boy threw popcorn at my head during lunch, but when I confronted him, he apologized, and insisted he'd been aiming for someone else.

Better yet, I'd successfully avoided Jackson all week. On Tuesday I saw him strut down the hall, and quickly ducked into the first open classroom. When he stopped by our table in the cafeteria to bum some money off Rachel on Wednesday, I hid behind a tree. Only Claire had noticed. In response to her quizzical glance, I'd crouched down and pawed at the ground. "I lost an earring," I'd told her. And she'd believed me, even though my ears aren't pierced. Sure, I felt kind of bad when she bent down to help me look for it, but not bad enough to tell her the truth.

I figured my problems were over.

But that was before Friday, when Mr. Beller passed back our book reports.

He waited until class was almost over before making the announcement. "I decided to be discreet, and write your grade on the last page, instead of the first," he explained, like he was doing us a huge favor. "That way you'll all have the opportunity to learn about your grade in private."

As soon as the first kid, Marco, got his book report back, he flipped to the last page, whooped, and yelled, "A-minus. Yes!"

So much for privacy. The more papers Mr. Beller passed out, the louder the room got. Kids yelled their grades across the room if they were happy with them, or just groaned loudly if they weren't. This happened despite our teacher's repeated requests to settle down.

No one listened. The room was pure chaos. I must say—all the frenzy got me excited. When I got my report, I anxiously flipped to the last page. Instead of a grade, I found a note written in red pen: *Annabelle, please see me after class. Mr. Beller.*

No one else got a note, as far as I could tell. I sat there in silence, trying to figure out what it could mean. Obviously, nothing good.

As soon as the bell rang I hurried up to Mr. Beller's desk.

"You wanted to see me," I said.

"Ah, yes, Annabelle with the ketchup stains." He chuckled to himself, like ketchup stains were extremely amusing. Then he folded his hands on his desk and sat back. "I'm concerned about the condition of your book report."

"Um, that wasn't really my fault."

I tried to explain but he cut me off, raising his hand and frowning, like he'd already heard all the excuses in the universe.

"I don't want to hear it. I just want a book report that doesn't smell like the cafeteria."

"Right, of course. I can get you a clean copy tomorrow. I was going to offer to do that last week, but—"

"It's too late for that," he said, shaking his head.

I looked from Mr. Beller to my book report, waiting for the obvious. But since he wasn't saying anything, I had to ask, "So, what's my grade?"

He sighed. "Clearly you read and understood the book. I can tell that you worked hard on this, which leaves me in a quandary. Had you turned in clean pages, you'd have gotten a B-plus. But since this is such a mess, well, I'm going to have to dock you a grade."

"A whole grade?" I cried. "You're giving me a C-plus?"

"I'm not giving you a C-plus. You've earned a C-plus."

I hated how he kept saying C-plus. And to get technical, I *earned* a B-plus. It's not like I asked Tobias and Erik to steal my report. None of this was my fault. "But that's not—"

"I don't want to hear it, Annabelle. Just don't let this happen again."

I stood there for a moment, my stomach in knots, trying to figure out a way to make him understand. But Mr. Beller had already slammed his grade book closed. He got up from his desk and began erasing the white board, like I wasn't even there. Clearly there was no reasoning with him.

I left the room in a daze. Anger burned inside of me. Confusion, too, because I didn't even know who to blame. Tobias? Mr. Beller? My mother for making me move to Westlake? Dweeble for dating my mom in the first place?

By the time I walked into social studies I was a few minutes late. My teacher, Ms. Winters, didn't say anything, but she did frown when I walked in, which was almost as bad.

We won our third basketball game in a row in PE, thanks to the free throws I made after Tommy fouled me. But it didn't help. I still felt lousy.

I couldn't even walk Pepper after school that day. When I peeked out the window, I saw Jackson dragging his skateboard ramp to the bottom of the cul-de-sac. I waited him out, hoping he'd get bored and go home. But five minutes later, four more boys I didn't recognize showed up. Each dressed almost identically in a ski cap, T-shirt, baggy shorts and Vans, like a uniform.

They stood around the ramp for a while, talking, shaking it, kicking the bottom, checking to make sure it was sturdy, I guess. Then they proceeded to skate off it, one by one.

Jackson alone was intimidating enough. But Jackson with four other guys? No way could I go near them. I didn't think so, anyway. And I certainly wasn't going to try.

Soon they moved on to more elaborate jumps. One kid did a three hundred and sixty degree turn in midair. The next one tried to do the same, but fell. As he rolled around on the street, cradling his knee in pain, his friends cheered and laughed.

Yup. You heard me right. He hurt himself and the other boys laughed!

I turned away from the window. This served as just one more example of how Jackson was like no dog I'd ever known or read about. In fact, putting Jackson in the same category as a dog insulted my dog in a major way. I loved Pepper. He was so much sweeter than Jackson, or any boy. It wasn't his fault he was out of control. It was just his natural puppy energy.

I think Pepper woke up every morning wondering,

"What kind of fun am I going to have today? Where will I get to go? Who will I jump all over? And which cool stuff will I chew up?"

Meanwhile, Jackson probably woke up asking, "Who am I going to torture today? And how?"

If my time at Birchwood taught me anything, it was this: Jackson was completely immune to training.

That got me thinking. What if only the sixth grade boys could be trained like dogs? In two years, they'd grow up to be eighth grade boys. And what would I do then?

Did it matter? Because even when my boy-training lessons worked, they didn't *really* work. Yes, I'd gotten my book report back after I stopped chasing Erik and Tobias. But they'd still managed to mess up my grade.

Maybe I just didn't belong at Birchwood. Maybe the universe was sending me a message.

I picked up the dog-training book, since there were still a few pages I hadn't yet read. But before I opened it, Pepper ran into my room, carrying one of Mom's sandals.

"Drop it, Pepper."

He ignored me, and stretched out on the floor so he could chew in a more comfortable position. I tried distracting him with Buttons but he wasn't interested.

"Drop it." I spoke sharply, which got him to stop, but only for two seconds. When I reached for the shoe, he pounced on it.

Great. That's just perfect. I'd been trying to get Pepper to drop things for weeks, and I wasn't getting anywhere. So if I can't even train my dog, what made me think I could ever train boys?

"Come on, Pepper." This time I waved Buttons in front of his face. "Mom got her fixed, so she's all in one piece."

He dropped the shoe and went for Buttons, but I put her on my highest bookshelf.

"Let's go, Pepper."

At least he followed me downstairs like I wanted him to.

Pepper went for the front door, but I had to take him out back, instead.

"Here, Pep."

I picked up an old tennis ball so we could play fetch. He'd finally gotten it down.

It would've been fun, had I not felt like we were under house arrest. Forced to stay in the backyard because I was too wimpy to go out front.

chapter eighteen
birthday bashing

I peeked out my bedroom window a few hours later to find the street empty. As happy as I was to see Jackson and the other skater guys gone, it didn't do me much good because it was already too late to take Pepper on a real walk.

At least I could go to Rachel's birthday party without stressing. She told me Jackson would be bowling all day, so I had nothing to worry about. I even found some real beach towels. Dweeble had a bunch left over from his first marriage. I took one with faded rainbow stripes. At first I was happy because it was cool and colorful, but as I walked across the street to Rachel's on Saturday, I worried that it looked too worn out. Hopefully, no one would care.

An older woman with short, curly dark hair and small glasses answered the door as soon as I rang the bell, like she'd been waiting in the entryway. "Oh, hi. You must be Annabelle. I'm Rachel's mom. Please call me Jenny. I'm so glad you're finally here. Isn't that always the way? The people who live closest are always the last to arrive." She spoke so quickly, it took me a few moments to take it all in.

"Hi, Jenny. Sorry." I didn't tell her why I was late. I'd been busy wrapping Rachel's present. I got her a silver charm bracelet with three charms I picked out myself—a purple flip-flop, a drum, and a birthday cake that said "Happy Birthday" across it in sparkly letters.

The problem was, I waited until this morning to wrap it, and couldn't get the bow right. I'd had to redo it three times. Obviously wrapping comes off fast and gets thrown away, but it seemed important to get it right. Especially since this was my first pool party. None of my friends from North Hollywood had their own pool.

Jenny took me to the back patio, which was decorated with pink and silver balloons and purple crepe paper. Everyone was hanging around the picnic table, snacking on chips and dip.

"Hey, Annabelle," they called.

"Hi, sorry I'm late." I set Rachel's present in the pile at the other end of the table.

"It's okay. Only Emma showed up at twelve fourteen," said Rachel.

"Actually, my dad dropped me off two minutes early but I waited outside until the exact moment," she explained.

"Does anyone need to change into their bathing suits?" Rachel's mom asked.

No one did. We'd all worn our swimsuits under our clothes, so we just got ready outside. Almost everyone had on one-piece suits like mine, which was a relief. Claire was the only one in a bikini and it was more of a tankini, anyway. Only about an inch of her stomach showed. We clumped together near the deep end and stared at the water.

When Rachel's mom came over with a camera, Rachel yelled, "Mom, stop!"

"I can't take pictures?" she asked.

"Not until we're in the water," Rachel said, turning away from her.

Her mom sat down at the picnic table, as the rest of us debated who should go in first.

"Rachel, I think you should because it's your birthday," said Claire.

"That's exactly why I shouldn't have to go."

"Well, someone has to," said Emma.

Since no one volunteered, we played princess, hunter, bear, which is like rock, paper, scissors, but more fun because you use your whole body, and not just your hands. To make a bear you throw your arms up over your head and growl. To be a princess, you put one hand on the back of your head, and one hand on your jutted-out hip. You can also pucker your lips and flutter your eyelids, if you really want to get into it. Being a hunter is easy. You just pretend you're pointing a rifle at someone.

Here's the ranking: bear eats the princess, princess conquers hunter, and hunter shoots the bear.

We played two people at a time until only Rachel and I were left.

In the final round, I was a hunter, and Rachel copped the princess pose, so she won.

I figured it was best to get the worst over with, so I took a running jump into the pool. The cold hit me fast. A chill zinged through my whole body.

"How is it?" Yumi asked.

My limbs felt numb, but I didn't admit that. Standing in the shallow end, I wrapped my arms around my body to keep from shivering. "Um, refreshing?"

"Yeah, right." Rachel dipped her toe in and said, "It's pu-pu-pu-positively fu-fu-fu-freezing."

When everyone else finally got in, Rachel's mom snapped some pictures and then told us to line up for swim races.

"Can't we just swim, for fun?" asked Rachel.

"Free swim will be in fifteen minutes," said her mom, holding up her stopwatch.

"How about ten?"

Her mom ignored her. "Does everyone know the breaststroke?"

Everyone giggled.

"I'll take that as a yes." She raised a red whistle to her lips.

Turns out we only had to go from one end of the pool to the other and back again. Rachel refused to participate and hopped onto a yellow inflatable raft instead. Claire said she wasn't into competitive sports, but she'd go along because she felt like swimming laps anyway, so that didn't leave many people for the race.

Emma and I tied for first place, but there wasn't any prize.

"Butterfly next," Rachel's mom announced. But then the doorbell rang, so she headed inside calling, "Be careful, girls. No roughhousing."

Once she was gone, Rachel swam for the steps, calling, "Everyone out of the pool, fast. I'm sick of racing."

We spread our towels out on the concrete and lay down.

Rachel passed around the sunblock. I was already slathered in my usual 45, but applied more anyway because the afternoon sun shined so bright. Everyone slipped on sunglasses. Since I'd forgotten mine, I closed my eyes.

"We need to figure out Halloween," said Rachel. "It's only four weeks away."

"Let's go as baseball players," said Yumi.

"You wanted to do that last year," said Claire.

"And we didn't."

"What if we dress like people from the eighties?" asked Emma.

"No, too many people are doing that," said Yumi.

"We can be sixties hippies," said Claire.

"But you dress like that every day," said Yumi, which was true. "Anyway, I think we should be some kind of group."

"What do you think, Annabelle?" asked Rachel.

I propped myself up on my elbows and squinted at her. "Last year, my friends and I went as the three musketeers."

"But that won't work because there are five of us," Emma pointed out.

This, I was happy to hear. Everyone knows Halloween is one of the most important holidays of the year. If Rachel's friends included me in their plans, it was like glue, cementing my place in their group. I thought so, anyway.

But then I realized that Sophia, Mia, and I had already planned our costumes over the summer. We were going to be the three blind mice. Of course, we never talked about Halloween at last weekend's sleepover, so maybe Mia and Sophia didn't want to dress up with me anymore. Maybe they'd changed their minds and were going as cowgirl twins instead. It made me a little sad to think about, but I felt more excited about trick-or-treating here with my new friends.

"How about school supplies?" asked Rachel.

We all looked at each other, waiting for someone to protest, but no one did.

"I like it," said Claire. "I think I'll go as a green highlighter. Or maybe one of those pens that writes in five different colors."

"It was eraser day at the Dodger-Yankee game last weekend and I have this pink eraser that says Dodgers," said Yumi. "I can make a life-size one. That counts, right?"

"Sure," said Rachel.

"Yes!" Yumi pumped her fist.

"Whatever we do, we have to make sure our costumes are Jackson-proof," said Claire.

"Yeah, I don't want to repeat last year's nightmare," Emma said.

Just hearing his name made me feel queasy. I couldn't even say it out loud, which meant that Jackson was my Voldemort, basically. I was almost afraid to ask but had to know. "What happened?"

Rachel explained. "Last year we went as fruit. I was a banana, Claire was a bunch of grapes, Yumi was an apple, and Emma—what were you, Emma?"

"A star fruit," said Emma. "Except no one realized. They just thought I was dressed as some weird star-shaped thing."

"We all met here before trick-or-treating, but Jackson was over with some of his friends. They didn't even have real costumes but they said they were blenders, which meant they surrounded us and started pushing us around."

"So they could make fruit shakes," Claire explained. "I told them there's no such thing as grapes in a fruit shake but they didn't care. My costume was made out of purple balloons and a bunch of them popped."

"They ripped the stem off my apple," said Yumi. "Rachel's mom taped it back on, but it wasn't the same."

I knew Rachel thought her brother was annoying,

but I hadn't realized Jackson was mean to her other friends, too. It didn't make me feel better, exactly, but it did make me feel less freakish.

If it happened to everyone, I wondered if maybe I was making too big a deal out of his teasing. Claire and Yumi seemed annoyed, but they didn't let Jackson ruin their lives. Maybe I could learn to ignore him. At least, that's what I was thinking when I heard a yell as loud and as fierce as a war cry.

I opened my eyes in time to see Jackson running toward us, clad in green swim shorts. He took a flying leap, hugged his knees to his chest, and cannonballed into the pool, soaking every single person around. Lucky me—I happened to be the closest, so I got more drenched than anyone. Well, except for Jackson, but he doesn't count. Clearly he wanted to be wet.

"Jackson!" Rachel screamed.

But he ignored her. Popping back onto the surface, he started kicking and splashing—not because he wanted to get to the other end of the pool in any hurry—just because he was intent on soaking us.

My towel got drenched.

"MOM!" Rachel yelled, running inside.

"Crybaby," Jackson called. He swam laps, kicking wildly—especially when he passed by us.

No one else at the party knew what to do. We all just sat there, blinking at one another in surprise-annoyance. But that didn't make me feel any better. Or less wet.

Rachel came back outside, looking plenty mad. "Mom says you have to stop splashing."

"I'm just swimming. It's not my fault your friends are too close to the pool."

"Why are you here, anyway?" she asked.

"I came home early because I didn't want to miss your party."

"But you weren't even invited. That's the whole point," said Rachel.

"Well, I'm here now." Jackson shrugged. Looking around, he narrowed his eyes at me. Then he raised his nose and started sniffing around. "Hey, what's that smell?" he asked.

Uh-oh.

Rachel seemed confused. "I don't smell anything."

I felt a familiar sinking feeling in the pit of my stomach. This always happened when Jackson was near.

Be strong. Don't show fear.

Yeah, right. This was hopeless. Jackson was the dominant dog, no question. And me? I didn't even qualify to be a submissive dog. I was more like some flea buzzing around him: a small but completely harmless nuisance.

Jackson treaded water and looked around in disgust, like he was suddenly surrounded by sewage sludge. "Hey, it's really warm in the pool. Did someone pee in here? Spazabelle?"

That's not my name, I thought.

Speak firmly, I told myself, but couldn't manage to open my mouth.

"The water is freezing and no one thinks you're funny," Rachel informed him.

Jackson climbed out of the pool and stood over me, blocking my sun and dripping more water on my already-soaked towel.

"Do you mind?" I finally managed.

"Do you mind not peeing in my pool?" he asked, and then cracked up, as if he'd said something funny, which he hadn't. Not at all.

The other girls stood and moved away, wrapping their bodies up in towels. This must be why Rachel told us to bring beach towels. They were big enough to hide in, in case her brother came around. Except mine was so soaked it was too heavy to lift.

As I watched him, something occurred to me. If Jackson were my dog, it'd be time to send him back to the shelter. Unfortunately, that wasn't an option.

"You're not funny," I said, standing up.

Jackson smirked at me. "No kidding, but at least you're admitting it."

"I didn't say that."

"But you didn't deny it."

"Yes I did."

"Oh, so now you're finally admitting that you peed in the pool. You're a pisser and a liar. And you crank called our house last week." He turned to Rachel. "You didn't know that, huh?"

"No. I, no." Tears pricked the corners of my eyes.

"Are you going to cry about it?" Jackson laughed meanly.

I took a deep, steady breath, but couldn't calm down. Rage churned from deep within me. It was too much. These past few weeks had been horrible—the worst of my life, probably. But it wasn't about Birchwood, or my lab partners, or the Corn Dog Boys, or Mr. Beller. No, most of that I could deal with.

There was more to it. A lot more. Jackson had made me miserable from day one. Jackson was out of control. Jackson was completely un-trainable. And now he was teasing me in front of all my new friends. But that didn't mean I had to sit there silently and take it.

"Why don't you just leave me alone. Leave us all alone. We were having a great time until you showed up and ruined everything, acting like some wild, out-of-control DOG!"

I didn't mean to scream that last bit, but once I did I had to admit, it felt pretty great.

Jackson narrowed his eyes at me. "What did you call me?" he asked.

"A dog!" I yelled. "You're a dog, Jackson."

I braced myself, in fear of retaliation. But Jackson seemed too stunned to say a word.

I heard laughter from behind me, which embarrassed me, until I realized Rachel's friends weren't laughing at me. No. That was the cool thing. They were laughing at Jackson.

It was weird, that moment. I felt stronger. Bigger, too. Like maybe things could be different around here.

Turning to face Jackson, I squared off my

shoulders. I didn't just look him in the eye. I stared him down. He seemed pretty surprised, and angry, too. For a few moments, he just stood there, blinking at me. Then rather than fight back, he stormed off, mumbling something about Rachel's stupid friends, and how he just wanted to go for a swim.

Once he was gone, the laughter died down and everyone got really quiet.

Rachel met my gaze and I held my breath. Her face was impossible to read, with her lips slightly parted and her eyes kind of bugging.

Had I gone too far? Was she mad that I'd called her brother a dog?

"Um, sorry," I whispered.

"Are you kidding?" she asked, finally cracking a smile. "That was awesome."

We high-fived, and then everyone surrounded me, all talking at once.

"That was amazing."

"So perfect."

"How'd you get rid of him?"

"Yeah, how?"

"Annabelle is just good at stuff like that," said Rachel.

The others nodded in agreement.

"Good at what?" I asked.

"Dealing with boys," Emma said.

"You're kidding, right? That was a fluke thing. Jackson makes me so nervous. Pretty much every boy at Birchwood does." I'd been so embarrassed, all this time, but it felt good to finally admit it. "They're like, a different species."

"Exactly. It's like you said. They're dogs," said Emma. "And speaking of, you got the Corn Dog Boys to move at lunch."

"And you told off Tobias," Claire said.

"I wish I could do that," said Rachel.

"Tobias bugs you, too?" I asked.

Rachel shook her head. "Not Tobias. This guy Will, from band. He's the other drummer and he's always telling me I should switch to the violin. So rude!"

"That's nothing compared to Jake, this guy in my French class," said Emma. "He asked to copy my homework on Friday and when I refused he called me a spaz."

They watched me eagerly, as if I had all the answers and could actually help. I didn't know what to tell them. But wait a second. "*I'm* the spaz," I said. "Random boys have been calling *me* that from day one."

"Me, too," said Yumi.

"Lots of sixth graders are called spazzes," Rachel said. "It's just some dumb Birchwood tradition. It used to be something the eighth graders called the new kids, but now even some sixth graders call each other spaz."

"I thought it was just me," I said.

Claire shook her head. "No, *you're* the only one who managed to get them to stop. I saw you in the hallway last week. You went up to that eighth grader and told him to cut it out."

"Amazing!" Yumi marveled.

"So, tell us how you did it," said Rachel.

"Um. Well, it started out as an accident . . ."

I told them about Pepper, and how I'd used his puppy-training lessons on boys. They couldn't believe it, and insisted on proof. I explained dog-speak, and then told them how important it was to act like the dominant dog in the pack.

"What else?" asked Emma. "I feel like I should be taking notes."

"Yeah, this is good stuff," said Claire.

"Can you help me get my brother to beg for treats and roll over?" asked Rachel.

We exploded into giggles.

"Probably not," I said. "But I'll bring the book to school on Monday."

Emma said, "You should open up a boy-training school."

"I know lots of girls who'd sign up," said Yumi.

Just then Rachel's mom came outside with a large pizza and a six-pack of soda, so we changed the subject. After lunch, we had ice cream cake, and Rachel opened up her presents, and then we swam some more.

And Jackson didn't bug us once.

chapter nineteen
boys, basketball, and bribes

When I finally made my way home, I was so tired I hardly noticed Dweeble playing basketball in our driveway. I'd forgotten he was coming home today. I didn't want to be rude, but I wasn't in the mood to talk, so I said a quick hello and marched right past him on my way to the front door.

"Hey, Annabelle," he called.

I froze with my hand on the doorknob. Something was up. Turning around, I walked back to the driveway and stared.

Dweeble was shooting hoops.

Dweeble *could* shoot hoops because we had a basketball hoop hanging above the garage.

I watched him, speechless.

"So, what do you think?" He palmed the ball. His hand was big enough to hold it like a pro ball player would.

"Um, when did you? Where? You just got this?"

Dweeble let out a big and loud belly laugh. "I wish your mom was home because she'd love to see your face right now."

"I didn't think we were getting a hoop," I said.

"You thought wrong. We bought it months ago, but it's been on back order until yesterday. I put it up as soon as I got home."

I stared at the hoop—at my hoop. Dweeble flew home from Switzerland and put up the hoop right away. How cool was that? But wait. He seemed too pleased with himself, which annoyed me. I wanted to be excited about the whole thing, but for some reason, I couldn't be.

"How was Switzerland?" I asked, stalling.

"Phenomenal. Beautiful country. Jason and I skied almost every day. He says hi, by the way. He'll probably be in town for Christmas and he's looking forward to meeting you. Oh, and I brought you back some chocolate—a different kind. Wait till you try it. It's amazing, and you can't even get it over here. So do you want to shoot, or what?" Dweeble offered me the ball, like it was nothing. Easy. Too easy. Like he thought he could just get me enough stuff, and everything would be fine. And not just fine, but good.

That's when I realized something crazy. Dweeble was assuming that I'd respond to treats, like Pepper did. Which meant he was trying to bribe me like I'd been trying to bribe the Birchwood boys.

But it wasn't just him. My own mother had been treating me like a dog, too. And suddenly I realized why it hadn't worked. I mean, it had a little, but not when it really mattered.

Some things are just bigger, and not everything can be fixed with treats. Sometimes it takes a lot more.

"You can't bribe me into liking it here."

Dweeble tucked the ball under his arm asking, "Huh?"

"The dog, the basketball hoop, the chocolate. I know what you're trying to do and it's not gonna work."

"Did something happen over at Rachel's?" he asked, glancing across the street, worried.

"No," I said. "Well, yes. Kind of. But that's not what this is about."

Dweeble bounced the ball. I watched him, not wanting to stay, but not wanting to go, either.

Finally, he said, "I'm sorry if you don't like it here, Annabelle. I hope that changes. We knew this move wouldn't be easy. And I guess if you want to be cynical, you can call this hoop a bribe, but I promise you, that's not how it was intended."

He sounded sincere but I wasn't about to give in that easily. "So, how else am I supposed to see it?"

"Well, when your mom and I decided to share our lives together, we wanted to be fair to you, too. We're just trying to make things good for you. Nicer, anyway. I know it's not easy and we can't fix everything, but we're doing what we can."

Dweeble dribbled the ball to the end of the driveway and shot a three-pointer. He missed, but just barely. "Anyway, you're not the only one who wanted a basketball hoop. So do you want to play?"

"No thanks." I wasn't ready to forgive him, but I wasn't ready to go inside, either, so I sat down on the front lawn and watched Dweeble play. He wasn't half bad. He could even slam-dunk. Of course, if I were over six feet tall, I'd be able to dunk too, probably.

A few minutes later, he set the ball down on the grass and told me he was going for a run. So predictable.

"Maybe we can shoot around a bit when I get back? Your mom tells me you're quite the player."

"Maybe."

"Okay, then. See you soon."

"Have fun," I called, and I think I might have meant it, even.

I watched Dweeble turn the corner, out of sight, then stared at the ball, itching to play. When I picked it up, the pebbly leather felt good against my skin. I tossed the ball from one hand to the other, keeping it light on my fingertips. Then I dribbled in place a bunch of times, loving the hollow, smacking sound. Finally, I went in for a lay-up. The ball swished through the hoop—a perfect shot.

I jumped up to get the rebound and slipped on the way down, landing on my butt. Youch! It's because my flip-flops had no grip. I stood up and wiped the loose gravel off the back of my shorts.

Then I ran after the ball, which was rolling toward the gutter. I picked it up and set it down on the lawn, then went inside for my high tops. They were buried underneath a bunch of clothes on my closet floor. Lucky for me, Pepper hadn't found them yet. It felt good, slipping them on and tying the laces.

Before I headed downstairs, I heard something from outside: the dreaded sound of wheels rolling on concrete. I peeked out my window and spotted Jackson skating up and down the street.

Figures he'd have to go and ruin my good time.

Telling him off in front of a huge crowd of friends was one thing. But facing him one-on-one? No way could I do it.

I sank down onto my bed, unable to believe my rotten luck. Even after all the work I'd done, it was like nothing had changed. I didn't want to wimp out, but I couldn't make myself go outside. So here I was again, trapped in my room.

Since I didn't have any other ideas, I reached for the dog-training book and flipped to the next lesson.

🐾 THE FINAL FRONTIER 🐾

Notice anything weird about all this dog training you've been doing? No? Then you're not thinking hard enough. Let's review the facts: if you've gotten this far, your dog can walk on a leash, heel, sit, stay, and fetch. Your dog also knows his or her name. And you've become the dominant dog in the pack. Right?

I nodded yes even though the book couldn't see me. This whole Jackson situation had gotten me so riled up, I was trying to interact with inanimate objects. As if I didn't have enough to worry about.

> Ask yourself, how did you manage to do all this? By training your dog? Okay, this is partly true. But you know what? Before you trained your dog you had to train yourself. Your dog needed a leader and you became that leader. So congratulations. The transformation is complete.

Okay, that lesson was a waste of time. Obviously I hadn't transformed into any kind of leader. I flipped to the next page.

> What are you looking for? My work here is done.

I turned the page, again.

> Seriously. I've got nothing more to say.

The next page read, *told you so,* and then came the index. After that I found a list of recommended reading.

First up was the sequel to *Good Dog!* It was called *Great Dog! More Training Tips.*

I couldn't believe I'd have to buy a whole different book to figure out what to do. How unfair was that? I tossed the training guide aside and looked down at the street.

That's when I realized something. I couldn't be

trained like a dog, and neither could Jackson. But I couldn't spend my life in hiding, either. Things couldn't go on like this forever. Jackson wasn't going anywhere and eventually, I'd have to deal with him on my own.

I looked at the book again. *You've changed. The transformation is complete.*

No, I didn't exactly believe those words, but they didn't seem *completely* off base. I'd stood up to Jackson—something that had seemed impossible a few weeks ago. So yeah, maybe I had changed a little. And maybe it was time to change some more. Maybe the book could only take me so far and the rest I'd have to figure out on my own.

I walked downstairs and headed outside. So far so good. Jackson didn't even notice. Picking up the ball, I dribbled and shot and missed. I got the rebound and shot again. And this time I made it. I kept shooting and soon the rumbling got louder. Then it stopped completely. I felt someone's eyes on my back.

Taking a deep breath, I turned around. Jackson stood on the sidewalk in front of my driveway.

Arms crossed, he sneered at me. "That hoop is so dumb. It's not even regulation height."

I just shrugged, turned around, and shot. Luckily, I made the basket and the next one, too. Then I dribbled in for a layup. The ball hit the rim and bounced off.

"Hah!" said Jackson.

Whatever. I grabbed the ball and I threw it at him. "Think fast."

He flinched but caught it. "You want me to play on your stupid hoop?"

"Well, obviously you want to play or you wouldn't be here," I said.

Jackson opened his mouth to protest, but didn't argue. "Fine, whatever," he said, and shot and missed.

He glared at me angrily, like he was daring me to say something, but I didn't. Everyone misses sometimes. No big deal. I just caught the rebound and threw the ball back up.

"I'm not a dog, you know." He said it out of nowhere.

My back was to Jackson. I didn't want to turn around to face him, but I made myself. "Okay, you're not a dog," I said, looking him in the eye. "But sometimes you act like one. And not in a good way, either."

He didn't respond, and I didn't say anything more, but we shot around for a while—after the sun set and the streetlights switched on.

Jackson didn't laugh or sneer or call me Spaz or give me dirty looks. We just played in silence, like we didn't hate each other's guts.

It's funny. I knew I'd changed over these past few weeks, but now I realized that Jackson had, too, although I'm not sure why. Maybe he was impressed that I'd finally stood up for myself, or maybe he just wanted to use my new hoop. It didn't really matter. Things were different tonight. And they'd be different from now on. I'd make sure of it.

When Jackson's mom called him inside for dinner, he tossed me the ball and said, "See you, Spazabelle."

But for once he didn't say it in a mean way, so I just laughed and said, "See ya."

Then he turned around and jogged back home. I stayed outside, unable to wipe the smile off my face.

A few minutes later, a tall, glowing green blob turned the corner and jogged toward me. Dweeble. If this happened last week, I'd have joked, "He's such an eyesore in his glow-in-the-dark clothes."

But I couldn't say that now, because I didn't really mean it.

The thing is, there must be something good to all of Dweeble's brightness. Like how, even in the dark, he still stood out.

In fact, the closer he got the more I realized something. I was happy he was almost home.

"Hey, how was the run?" I asked.

"Glorious," he called, and stopped short at the bottom of the driveway. Holding up his hands he said, "Let's have it. I'm wide open."

I grinned and passed Dweeble the ball.

He charged forward and slam-dunked.

"Nice one," I said grabbing the ball before it bounced into the street. I tossed it to him again, thinking, *who knows*? Maybe someday I'd even start calling Dweeble Ted.

On the other hand, there's no point in getting carried away.

Acknowledgments

Special thanks to Julie Romeis, Michelle Nagler, Caroline Abbey, Melissa Kavonic, Nira Hyman, Nicole Gastonguay, Laura Langlie, Coe Booth, Sarah Mlynowski, Dan Ehrenhaft, Robin Wasserman, Ethan Wolff, Jessica Ziegler, Amanda McCormick, Emma Reuland, Sydney Foreman, and Jim Margolis

Think you've learned how to master those boys—er, dogs?

Get ready for a whole different breed of training in Annabelle's next adventure, ***Girls Acting Catty***

terrible T

When I got to PE on Monday, I sat down on the blacktop for roll call, as usual. We always line up in alphabetical order, which means that I sit right behind Taylor, because my last name is Stevens and hers is Stansfield. Usually I smile at her and she smiles back.

But ever since Halloween, I didn't know how to act. I wasn't going to *not* be nice to Taylor, just because Rachel and my other friends didn't like her. That wouldn't be fair. Sure, Taylor had been pretty mean to Rachel, but Rachel had been mean right back. I didn't know who started the whole thing, and I didn't want to get stuck in the middle or take sides.

Plus, Rachel was wrong. Taylor isn't ugly. She's actually really pretty with shiny dark hair and wide-set green eyes. Also, she's super outgoing. In chorus, she's always the first one to volunteer to do solos. She wants to be a pop star when she grows up, and she talks about it all the time. Rachel thinks this makes her obnoxious and snobby, but I think it's okay to have something you really, really want to do.

Rachel should agree. She's the one who wants to be a drummer in a rock band. So how is that any different? I'd asked her about it on Saturday night, but she didn't explain and I didn't push it.

To smile or not to smile—that was the question. Before I could decide, Taylor turned around and looked at me with a blank expression on her face, like she was just noticing I existed for the first time. That seemed a little weird, but then she did something really crazy. She panned my whole body, looking me up and down like I was a secondhand bike she was thinking about buying. When she finally finished, she looked disappointed and frowned like she thought I was used and damaged goods or something.

"What?" I shouldn't have asked, but the question came out before I could stop myself.

She scrunched her eyebrows together, as if she were thinking pretty hard, which got me all panicky. Like, maybe she found so many things wrong, she didn't even know where to begin.

When her gaze finally met mine she asked, "Your mom won't let you shave your legs yet, huh?"

I looked down at my legs, and she did too. I didn't know what to tell her, or even if I was supposed to give her an answer.

True, my legs are a little furry, but my hair is so pale you can hardly see it. There's no point in shaving. But what if every other sixth-grade girl at Birchwood already does? Maybe I'm the only holdout.

I'm not sure if Rachel or my other new friends shaved. We'd never talked about it before. Maybe they all did and thought I was weird and babyish for not doing it. Although they were my friends, and too nice to think of me that way. So maybe they didn't bring up shaving on purpose because they didn't want me to feel bad, which was worse.

I sat there dumbly, looking at my legs. Time seemed to slow to a crawl. Each agonizing second felt more like an hour.

Taylor stared at me, waiting for an answer. She didn't even blink.

Finally I said, "No." But even as the word came out of my mouth, I wished I'd had a better response.

Like, "I'm not sure, because I don't want to shave my legs yet, so I never bothered asking. But if I did, my mom would probably say go ahead, because she's cool about stuff like that."

That was the truth. But the truth didn't seem good enough. Of course, neither did the lie. Taylor turned back around and didn't say anything else to me for the rest of class.

Probably, she'd never speak to me again.

At this point, I kind of hoped not.

PE is my last class of the day, but I couldn't go right home when it ended because I had to meet Tobias and Oliver in the library after school. We're in the same lab group in science, and we'd spent the last two weeks growing mold spores on bread. Now we had to write up a lab report about the experiment. It was due on

Wednesday, and these reports counted for a big part of our grade, so we really had to get it right.

I just wished I had long pants to change into. I'd worn shorts to school and tennis shoes with no socks. Now I worried that everyone would notice my hairy calves and think I was a freak. It was entirely possible that I was the only girl at Birchwood Middle School who didn't shave. And until I knew for sure, I'd just have to be careful to keep my legs hidden.

When I got to the library, the boys were already there. Oliver is cute, with dirty blond hair shaved into a buzz cut, green eyes, and skin that's kind of dark because he's half black. He has a nice accent, which I never noticed before, because he hardly talks. But ever since he told me he was born in Jamaica and only moved to California four years ago, I always hear it. Tobias is pale, with shaggy dark hair and glasses and a big nose and pimples that creep from his cheeks down to his neck and disappear into his shirt collar. Basically, he's not so cute, but he seems to think he is.

Even though I was feeling lousy after the whole Taylor/leg-shaving thing, I stood up tall and swaggered over to them, throwing my backpack on the table and saying, "Hey, what's up?"

Then I pulled out my notebook and doled out the work before they had a chance to argue with me. "There are six sections in a lab, so let's split them up and each do two. Tobias, you can write the introduction and hypothesis. Oliver, you list the materials and supplies and then explain the procedure. And I'll write up our observations and the conclusion."

"How come you get to do the conclusion?" asked Tobias.

I crossed my arms over my chest and glared. "Do you want to do it? Because I don't really care."

"No, whatever. It's fine." Tobias pushed up his glasses, bent over his notebook, and started writing.

I had to smile. If someone didn't know better, they'd think I was pretty bossy, but I'm not. Really. It's all an act.

At the beginning of the school year, Oliver and Tobias hogged all the lab equipment and they never let me do anything, but then I used some of Pepper's dog-training lessons on them and things have been okay ever since. For everyone, I think. We finished writing up our lab in less than two hours. Then Oliver's mom drove us all home.

I was so glad to be back. At least, until I walked through the front door and heard loud voices coming from the kitchen.

"This isn't a big deal," Dweeble said. "I'm sorry, but I just assumed that you'd want to change your name when we got married. Traditionally—"

"When have I ever been traditional?" Mom asked. "And what about Annabelle? I can't have a different last name than my own daughter."

"You didn't let me finish. I was about to say that I never thought about that, but—"

"Well, you should have."

"There you go, interrupting me again."

Yikes. I froze, just inside the front door, not wanting to eavesdrop but too curious to move. I'd never heard Mom and Dweeble fight before, and wondered if they were breaking up. They'd have to call off the wedding. Then Mom and I might have to move back to North Hollywood. I'd just gotten used to things here, and I didn't want to move. Not even after the humiliation in gym class.

I opened the door again, and slammed it shut as hard as I could, yelling, "Hi, I'm home!"

They stopped talking immediately, and then a few seconds later my mom came into the entryway with a tight, forced-looking smile on her face. "Hi, Annabelle. Did you finish your book report?"

"It's a lab report," I replied. "Um, can I ask you something?" I needed to talk to her about shaving. Not only because of what happened in PE today, but also because I was curious. I wasn't *only* asking because of Taylor. "It's important," I said, making my way upstairs and hoping she'd come too.

"What is it?" She glanced toward the kitchen, distracted. I wasn't going to ask her out in the open, when Dweeble could walk in at any second. But she wasn't following me to my room. So instead, I asked her if I could go over to Rachel's.

Mom glanced at her watch. "That's fine, but don't stay for too long. Ted and I are making lasagna and it should be ready in about an hour."

I felt like asking her if "making lasagna" was some

new term for "yelling at each other," but I didn't want her to know I'd heard anything. So instead I said, "Okay." Then I dropped my backpack off in my room, changed into jeans, and headed across the street.

Jackson answered the door a minute after I knocked, asking, "What do you want?"

For once, I didn't blame him for being rude. He was probably still mad about Halloween. "Hey, Jackson. I just wanted to see if you needed to borrow my shampoo."

"Huh?" he asked.

"So you can wash all that rotten egg out of your hair. Remember? Or did Claire hit you too hard and give you amnesia?"

"Very funny," Jackson grumbled, and tried closing the door in my face.

I held it open. "No, wait. Sorry. I'm just kidding. Is Rachel home?"

Jackson rolled his eyes, but still turned around and yelled for her. "Hey, pizza face!"

I cringed. Poor Rachel. It was bad enough having bad acne, probably, without having some mean older brother making fun of her all the time.

Not that Rachel was going to sit there quietly and take it. "Shut up, egghead," she said, running downstairs. "Don't call me that."

"Why, are you going to tell on me?" Jackson asked, in a fake-whiny voice.

Rachel pushed past him. "Hey, Annabelle. Come on in."

She grabbed my arm and led me upstairs to her room.

"You are so lucky you're an only child," she said, slamming the door so we could have some privacy.

"Except I won't be for long. Pretty soon I'll have a stepbrother."

"But he's not going to live with you," said Rachel.

"He is for six weeks," I said. "Dweeble bought new sheets for the bed in the extra bedroom. In fact, he doesn't even call it the extra bedroom anymore. Suddenly it's Jason's room. And guess what else? When mini-Dweeb stays with us, I'm going to have to share a bathroom with him."

"Mini-Dweeb?" she asked.

"That's his new nickname. It's easier to say than 'son of the Dweeb.'"

"Good point." Rachel nodded. "But I really don't think you have to worry. Mini-Dweeb is in college, which means he's too grown up to make fun of you."

This made sense, but I hadn't come over to Rachel's house to talk about brothers—real or step. "Hey, do you shave your legs?" I asked.

"Yeah," said Rachel. "I started to this summer. How come?"

She sounded so casual about it, I almost regretted bringing it up. But it was too late. I had to know. I took a deep breath and asked, "Does everyone shave their legs? All our friends, I mean."

"Um, I know Emma does, but I don't think Claire and Yumi do. How come?"

"No reason," I said. "I was just wondering." And since she was looking at me kind of funny, I told her about what happened in PE.

Rachel freaked. "I can't believe Taylor said that to you! She's so horrible!"

I nodded. It felt good having Rachel leap to my defense so quickly. But at the same time, I didn't want to make *too* big a deal out of it.

"The thing is—I'm not positive she said it to be mean. She just sort of asked me, like she was wondering, but I don't know. It was weird . . ."

"Of course she said it to be mean," said Rachel. "That's what she's all about. Other people play instruments, or collect puffy stickers. Taylor's favorite pastime is making people feel bad about themselves. It's, like, a hobby for her. As if she's so perfect. Did you see her jeans today? They probably cost two hundred dollars, because she only wears designer clothes. But they look terrible. She should not be wearing low riders with her body because when she sat down, her shirt rode up and she had a total muffin top."

"Muffin top?" I asked.

"It's when your hips sort of swell and hang out of your jeans, like the top of a muffin."

I laughed. Sure it was mean, but it was still funny. And anyway, why should I feel bad when Taylor made me feel lousy on purpose?

"Her muffin top shows in her PE clothes too," I said. "And the other day, her underwear was sticking out of her shorts."

"No!" yelled Rachel.

"Seriously. They were pink with white stars."

"Stars?" asked Rachel. "Think she wore them because she's so convinced she's gonna be this huge star?"

We both giggled.

"She probably had them showing on purpose," Rachel said. "You know, to get attention. All her friends are like that. Don't you hate how they walk around school like they own it? They're the biggest snobs in the entire sixth grade and, like, proud of it."

I didn't know any of Taylor's friends except for Hannah, who I'd always liked. She and I sat next to each other in French. She's tall, with big brown eyes and straight, shoulder-length, dirty-blond hair that she constantly tucks and re-tucks behind her ears. Whenever we have to switch papers for grading in French, we choose each other. Last Tuesday, I got a hundred percent and she put a happy face by my score.

Snobby girls do not draw happy faces. It's a fact.

"Hannah seems okay," I said.

Rachel groaned. "Hannah is the worst! She pre-tends like she's all sweet and quiet, but it's just an act. Trust me. If she were nice, she wouldn't be friends with Taylor. Haven't you noticed how she follows her around and does whatever she wants like some clue-less, pathetic little puppet?"

I shrugged. "I guess I never really paid attention."

"Well, now that I pointed it out I know you'll

notice. And you cannot start shaving now, just because of what Taylor said."

I didn't know when I'd start shaving, but it didn't seem like the kind of thing Rachel should be able to decide for me. I mean, I'm glad she was on my side and everything, but she was acting weird—too angry for something that didn't even happen to her.

"But what if my legs are too hairy? People are noticing, obviously."

"Let's see."

I rolled up my jeans and Rachel leaned closer to inspect my calves. "Your hair is so pale, you can hardly see it."

"That's what I used to think."

"You know, once you start shaving you can never stop. Your hair won't be all soft and smooth like it is now."

"It won't?" I rolled my jeans back down and crossed my legs.

Rachel shook her head. "Nope. The razor cuts it at a different angle so it'll feel all stubbly. My mom waxes, but waxing looks like torture."

My only experience with wax involved wax lips, but somehow I doubted that's what Rachel was talking about. "What's waxing?" I asked.

"It's when they brush hot wax on your legs and then cover it with cloth. When the wax cools down it sticks to your hair and then they rip the cloth off really fast and it takes the wax and all your hair with it."

I gasped. "No!"

"Seriously. It's totally painful, because it rips the hair out from the follicles," Rachel explained. "But it lasts longer, for the same reason."

"It doesn't take your skin off with it?" I asked.

Rachel shook her head. "Nope. But I'd still never do it. Shaving is much better."

I didn't want to admit it out loud, but shaving didn't seem so much better to me. I know it's not supposed to hurt, but it still involves running a razor blade up your leg, and I just don't get how that can't be painful.

Ever notice how commercials for razor blades always feature some woman shaving in a gigantic tub filled with bubble bath? Well, bubble bath makes me sneeze. So what happens if I sneeze and slip and cut myself with the razor? I'd start to bleed, probably, and blood makes me squeamish. What if I'm bleeding and the sight of it makes me pass out? I could drown in my very own bathtub. That is not a good way to go. Not that there's any good way to go, but drowning in your own bathwater has got to be one of the worst.

I guess Rachel could tell I was stressing, because she said, "You don't need to shave. Just forget about Taylor. I wish we didn't have PE with her. I wish she didn't even go to our school."

"Yeah." I agreed because it was easier, but to be honest, Taylor hadn't ever really bugged me much before. Well, except for today. And on Halloween, I guess.

I wondered why Rachel hated Taylor so much,

but that wasn't something I could just ask her straight out.

On my way home, I had this weird thought. Maybe Taylor made me feel bad on purpose just because I was a part of Rachel's crowd. And as for all those times she'd been nice in the past? Maybe she hadn't noticed who my friends were.

Dweeble was just taking the lasagna out of the oven when I walked inside. He and my mom acted normal for the rest of the night, so either they'd made up or they were really good at faking getting along.

As I got ready for bed, I realized I'd forgotten to ask Rachel not to say anything to our other friends. About the whole Taylor/shaving thing, I mean. I didn't want it to turn into a big deal, nor did I want to advertise that I hadn't started shaving, but it was too late to call her. And by the time I saw her again, she'd already spilled the beans.

At school the next morning I found all my friends huddled around my locker. As soon as I was close enough, Emma said, "I can't believe Taylor said that to you."

I looked from her to Rachel to Claire to Yumi. "What's going on?" I asked, although I already had a pretty good idea.

"I told them how Terrible T made fun of you for not shaving," said Rachel.

"She didn't make fun of me exactly," I said as I worked the combination on my locker. "It was more like, well, more like she just asked me but it was weird."

"No, she did it on purpose," said Rachel. "And that's just like her."

"Rachel's probably right," said Emma. "But don't worry about it."

"Yeah, I don't shave my legs yet," said Claire.

"And neither do I," said Yumi.

"I just started last summer," said Emma. "But it's not a big deal."

I was glad to have everyone on my side—but I still felt self-conscious. I wore jeans to school, and socks with my tennis shoes, even though it was pretty hot out. I told myself I wasn't hiding my legs. But deep down, I knew the truth. Hopefully my friends wouldn't make the connection, though. Of course, it would be even worse if Taylor realized it. But what other choice did I have?

"Does her underwear really stick out of her gym shorts every day?" asked Yumi.

"Not every day." I glanced at Rachel, who looked away. "I never said every day."

"Still, it's pretty gross," said Emma.

"*She's* gross, so it's fitting," Rachel said with a huff. "Sure she thinks she's all that, but she's really just a giant muffin top wrapped in designer clothes."

"Oh, so fierce!" said Claire. Claire had been calling lots of things fierce, ever since she heard the word on *Project Runway*, her favorite show. As far as I could tell, it could mean awesome, nasty, or way harsh, depending on the context.

Just then I noticed Hannah and Taylor walking

toward us. Yumi saw them too, and told us all to shush, which we did.

As soon as they passed us by, Claire whispered, "Fierce!" and the rest of us exploded into laughter. We just couldn't help ourselves.

I guess we were pretty loud because both Hannah and Taylor glanced over their shoulders. Obviously, they knew something was up, but I figured I was safe. No way could Taylor know we were laughing at her.

Still, our eyes met for a brief second and this look of anger flashed over her face. Like somehow she'd figured it out. The thought gave me the chills.

Later on I tried smiling at Taylor in the hallway, like everything was still cool. She just looked away, as if she didn't even know me.

Then when we had to exchange homework in French, Hannah traded papers with Morgan Greely instead of me. I had to switch with Jeremy Lundy, who marked my mistakes with gigantic red x's, leaving my paper a huge mess even though I'd only gotten two answers wrong.

I felt nervous walking into chorus, but I told myself there wasn't any need to. No way could Taylor and Hannah suddenly not like me just because they assumed my friends and I were laughing at them. Okay, true, we were. But they had no way of knowing that. They couldn't have heard our conversation or anything.

Still, as soon as I headed to my seat, Hannah and

Taylor looked at each other and laughed. Then when I glanced at them they grinned, but in this evil "we know something you don't know" kind of way.

An ice-cold, icky feeling spread through me. Obviously Hannah and Taylor had been talking about me. But were they saying something about my legs? Or my friends? Or worse?

Half of me was dying to know.

And the other half was scared to find out.

Jimmy Bruch

leslie margolis lives in Brooklyn, New York, with her fairly well-trained, six-toed mutt named Aunt Blanche and her less well-trained husband, Jim. She is also the author of *Girls Acting Catty* and the young adult novels *Fix* and *Price of Admission*. Visit her online at www.lesliemargolis.com.